Press Minerva

The Fairiest or Surprising and Entertaining Adventures of the Aerial Beings

In Which are Related Several Uncommon Tales

Press Minerva

The Fairiest or Surprising and Entertaining Adventures of the Aerial Beings
In Which are Related Several Uncommon Tales

ISBN/EAN: 9783337026479

Printed in Europe, USA, Canada, Australia, Japan

Cover: Foto ©Andreas Hilbeck / pixelio.de

More available books at **www.hansebooks.com**

THE

FAIRIEST;

OR

SURPRISING AND ENTERTAINING

ADVENTURES

OF THE

ÆRIAL BEINGS;

IN WHICH ARE RELATED SEVERAL

UNCOMMON TALES	STRANGE METAMORPHOSES
WONDERFUL STORIES	DANGEROUS ESCAPES
CURIOUS ACCIDENTS	AND HAPPY CONCLUSIONS;

THE WHOLE SELECTED TO

AMUSE AND IMPROVE JUVENILE MINDS.

Here Vice and Virtue you may fee,
Painted in their juft Degree.

LONDON:

PRINTED FOR WILLIAM LANE,

AT THE

Minerva-Prefs,

LEADENHALL-STREET.

M DCC XCV.

For the Defcription of the elegant Frontifpiece,
fee Page 20.

THE
FARIEST.

THE

STORY

OF

FORTUNIO,

THE

FORTUNATE KNIGHT.

THERE once reigned a powerful king, who was a prince of great clemency, and very well beloved by his fubjects; but being engaged in a war with an emperor, whofe name was Matapa, a neighbouring and potent prince, after 'feveral battles, the emperor at laft gained an entire and fignal victory. The king had moft of his officers and foldiers killed, or taken prifoners, and the emperor foon after befieged his capital town, and took it; by which means he became mafter of all the treafures. The king had much ado to efcape himfelf, with the queen dowager, his fifter, who was young, beautiful, and witty, but withal proud, hafty, and difficult of accefs. The emperor tranfported all his jewels and rich furniture to his own palace, and took a great number of young damfels, horfes, and whatever might be ufeful and agreeable to him; and when he had de-

A 2 populated

populated the greateſt part of the kingdoms, returned in triumph home, where he was received by the empreſs and the princeſs his daughter, with all the joy imaginable; while the dethroned king endured, with the utmoſt impatience, his misfortunes. He aſſembled what troops he had left, formed a ſmall party, and to augment it as ſoon as poſſible, publiſhed an ordinance, requiring all gentlemen, who were his ſubjects, either to come and ſerve him in their own proper perſons, or to ſend one of their ſons well mounted and armed.

There lived on the frontiers an old lord, who had ſeen full fourſcore years, and was a man of extraordinary parts, but had partaken ſo much of the frowns of fortune; that he was very much reduced, and had bore all his ill fortune with more patience, had not three beautiful daughters ſhared it with him. But as they were women of good ſenſe, they never murmured at their misfortunes, but rather, when they ſpoke, comforted their father, than added to his afflictions. In this manner they lived with him in an old country-houſe, free from ambition, when this ordinance reached the old gentleman's ear; who called his daughters, and, with a countenance that diſcovered the grief of his mind, ſaid to them, ' What ſhall we do? The king has or-
' dered all perſons of diſtinction in his dominions to
' ſerve him againſt the emperor, or pay ſuch a fine,
' which I am not able to do; and theſe extremities will
' either coſt me my life, or be our ruin.' His three daughters were as much concerned as himſelf at this news, but yet deſired him not to be diſheartened, ſince they were perſuaded ſome remedy might be found out. The next day, the eldeſt went to her father, as he was walking melancholy in his little orchard, and ſaid to him, ' I come my lord, to entreat you to let me go to
' the army; I am of an advantageous height enough,
' and robuſt: I will dreſs myſelf in men's cloaths, and
' paſs for your ſon: If I do no heroic actions, I ſhall
' however ſave you a journey or the tax, which is a great
' deal in our circumſtances.' The count embraced her tenderly, and at firſt oppoſed ſo extraordinary a deſign;
but

but she reprefented to him, with great firmnefs of mind,
that there was no other expedient, and thereby got his
confent.   Her father provided cloaths and arms for her,
and gave her the beft of four horfes, which he kept to
go to plow and cart, and after the moft tender farewell
on both fides, fhe fet out on her journey.   After fome
days travel, as fhe paffed by a large meadow, befet
with a quickfet hedge, fhe faw a fhepherdefs very much
grieved, who was endeavouring to pull a fheep out of
a ditch: ' What are you doing there fhepherdefs?' (faid
' fhe) ' Alas! (replied the fhepherdefs) I am ftriving
' to fave a fheep that is almoft drowned, and am fo
' weak, that I cannot draw him out.'   ' I pity you,'
(faid fhe,) and, without offering her affiftance, rid away.
Whereupon the fhepherdefs cried out, ' Good-bye,
' difguifed fair.'   Which put our heroine into an inexpreffible furprife.   ' How is it poffible, (faid fhe to
' herfelf) that I fhould be known? This old fhepher-
' defs has but juft fet eyes on me, and has difcovered
' what I am; what fhall I do? I fhall be known to all
' the world, and how afhamed and vexed fhall I be, if the
' king fhould find me out! He will think my father a
' coward, that durft not expofe himfelf to danger.'
At laft fhe concluded to go home again.

The count and his daughters were talking of her, and
reckoning how long fhe had been gone, when they faw
her come in, who told them her adventure.   The good
old count faid it was nothing but what he forefaw; that
if fhe would have taken his advice, fhe had not gone,
becaufe he thought it impoffible but fhe muft be difcovered.   This little family was embarraffed again,
when the fecond daughter faid to her father, ' I am
' not furprifed that my fifter fhould be difcovered, fince
' fhe never was on horfeback before; but for my part,
' if you will let me go in her ftead, I dare promife, you
' fhall not need to repent it.'   It was in vain for the
old count to refufe her; he was forced to confent, and
fhe took other cloaths and arms, and another horfe;
and when fhe was thus equipped, embraced her father
and fifters, and refolved to ferve the king; but as fhe

paffed

paſſed by the ſame meadow, ſhe ſaw the ſame ſhepherdeſs drawing a ſheep out of a deep ditch, who cried out,
' Unfortunate wretch that I am, to loſe half my flock in'
' this manner; if any body would help me, I might
' ſave this poor creature.' ' What! ſhepherdeſs (cried
' out this ſecond daughter) do you take no better care
' of your ſheep, than to let them fall into the water?'
Then ſpur'd on her horſe, and rid away. ' Farewell,
diſguiſed fair,' (cried the old woman to her.) Which
words were no ſmall affliction to our Amazon. ' How
' unfortunate (ſaid ſhe) is it to be thus known: 'I have
' no better luck than my ſiſter: It will be ridiculous for
' me to go to the army with ſuch an effeminate air.'
Thereupon ſhe returned home very much vexed at her
bad ſucceſs.

The old count received her with a great deal of tender-
neſs, and commended her prudence, but could not help
being chagrined at the expence he had been at, of two
ſuits of cloaths and other things, though he concealed it
as much as poſſible from his daughters.   At laſt the
youngeſt daughter deſired him, with the moſt preſſing
inſtances to give her leave, as he had done both her ſiſ-
ters. ' Perhaps (ſaid ſhe) you may think it preſump-
' tion in me to think to ſucceed better than they, yet I de-
' ſire I may try; I am ſomewhat taller than they; you
' know I have been uſed to hunting, which exerciſe bears
' parrallel with war; and my great deſire to comfort
' you in your misfortunes, will inſpire me with extra-
' ordinary courage.'   As the count loved this daughter
better than the other two, becauſe ſhe always took moſt
care of him, and read to divert him, and killed game
for him; he uſed all the arguments he was maſter of,
to diſſuade her from her deſign. ' If you leave me,
' my dear child (ſaid he) your abſence will be my
' death; for ſhould fortune favour you in your under-
' taking, and you ſhould return crowned with laurels,
' I ſhall not have the pleaſure of ſeeing it, ſince I am in
' ſo advanced an age.' ' No father (ſaid ſhe) do not
' think the time long, the war muſt ſoon be at an end;
' and if I find out any other way to fulfil the king's
                                                    orders,

' orders, I will not neglect it: for I can assure you, if,
' my absence is a trouble to you, it is no less to me.'
By these words she at last persuaded him into a consent;
and after that made up a plain suit of cloaths, for her
sisters had exhausted the old count's treasures too much
for her to have any better; and was forced to take up
with one of the worst horses, because the others were,
lamed: but all this could not discourage her: She embraced her father, asked his blessing, and after shedding
some tears with him and her sisters, set forwards on her,
journey.

As she went by the same meadow, she saw the old,
shepherdess endeavouring to pull the sheep out of a ditch.
' What are you doing there, shepherdess?' (said she.),
' I have been doing, Sir, (replied the old woman) till
' l can do no longer: I have been ever since the break
' of day striving to get this sheep out, and all to no pur-
' pose; and I am so weary I can scarce stand: there is
' never a day passes over my head but some misfortune
' attends me, and nobody will help me.' ' Indeed I
' pity you (said our young warrior) and to shew it the
' more, will assist you.' Thereupon alighted from her
horse, and jumping over the hedge, she went into the
ditch, where she worked till she got this favourite sheep
out. ' Do not cry, shepherdess (said she) here is your
' sheep; and considering the time he has lain in the
' water, he is very brisk.' ' You shall not find me un-
' grateful, charming maid, (said the shepherdess) I
' know where you are going and all your designs; your
' sister passed by this meadow, I knew them and their
' thoughts; but they were so hard-hearted and unkind,
' that I found the means to prevent their journey; but
' for your part, you shall find it otherwise. I am a
' fairy, and have a great inclination to reward
' those that are deserving. That horse you ride is but
' a poor sorry one, I will give you a better.' Thereupon striking the ground with her crook, our warrior
heard a whinnying behind a holt of trees, and presently
saw a beautiful horse gallopping about the meadow. The
fairy called this courser to her, and touching him with

A 4   her

her crook, faid, faithful Comrade, be accoutered finer
than the beft horfe of the Emperor Metapa; and immediately Comrade had on a faddle and houfing of green
velvet embroidered with diamonds, a bridle ftrung with
pearls, with boffes and bit of gold.

' What you fee (faid the fairy) is the leaft thing you
' ought to admire this horfe for; he has a great many
' rare qualities which I will inform you of. Firft, he
' eats but once in eight days: and then he knows what
' is paft, prefent, and to come: for I have had him a
' long time, and brought him up to my hand. When
' you want to be informed of any thing, or are at a lofs
' for advice, you muft addrefs yourfelf to him, and muft
' look on him more like your friend than a horfe. Be-
' fides, I do not like your habit, I will give you one
' fhall pleafe you better.' Then ftriking on the ground
with her crook, there arofe up a turkey leather trunk,
adorned with nails of gold; the fairy looked on the
grafs for the key which opened it: It was lined with
fpanifh leather embroidered, and contained a dozen
complete fuits of clothes, with dozens of all appurtenan-
ces, as fwords, linen, &c. The cloaths were fo rich with
embroidery and diamonds that our Amazon could hardly lift them. The fairy bid her chufe which fhe liked
beft, and told her the reft fhould follow her wherever fhe
went; and that fhe needed but to ftamp with her foot,
and call for her turkey-leather trunk, and it fhould come
to her full of money and jewels, or full of fine linen and
laces, which fhe called for, either into her chamber or
in the field. ' But, (faid the Fairy) you muft make
' choice of fome name agreeable to your profeffion; and
' I think you may call yourfelf Fortunio: Befides, I
' think it not improper you fhould know me in my
own perfon.' At that very moment fhe caft off her old
fkin, and appeared fo beautiful that fhe dazzled the eyes
of our young heroine. Her habit was blue velvet lined
with ermine, her hair was platted with pearls, and on
her head ftood a ftately crown. Our young warrior was
fo tranfported with admiration, fhe caft herfelf at her
feet, fo great was her acknowledgment. The fairy
raifed

raifed her up, and embraced her tenderly, and bid her take a habit of gold and green brocade, which she accordingly obeyed, and mounted her horfe, continued on her journey, fo penetrated with the extraordinary fortune she had met with, that she could think of nothing elfe   She examined with herfelf by what good fortune she had gained the good will of fo powerful a fairy; for she faid to herfelf, ' She could with one ' ftroke of her wand have drawn out, without my affift- ' ance, a whole flock from the center of the earth.   It ' was fortunate for me I was fo ready to oblige her; she ' knew the fentiments of my heart, and approved of ' them.   If my father faw me now fo rich, and in all ' this magnificence, how overjoyed would he be, and ' how well pleafed should I be to have my family par- ' takers with me !'

As she made an end of thefe reflections, she arrived at a great city, and drew on her the eyes of all the people, who followed and crowded about her, faying, they never faw fo fine and handfome a knight, and fo graceful a horfe before.   She had all manner of refpects paid to her, which she returned with all imaginable civility.   As foon as she came to an inn, the governors, who had feen her as he was walking out, and admired her, and fent a gentleman to defire her to accept of an apartment in his caftle.   Fortunio, for fo we muft call her, anfwered, that as he had not the honour to be known to him, he would not take that freedom, but would come and pay his refpects to him; but withal defired he would let him have a trufty fervant to fend to his father; which the Governor did inftantly, and our knight defired him to come again that night, becaufe his difpatch- es were not ready.   He shut himfelf up faft in his cham- ber, then ftamping with his foot, and calling for the Turkey leather trunk full of diamonds and piftoles, it appeared that moment; but then he was at a lofs for the key, and knew not where to find it, and thought with himfelf it would be a thoufand pities to break open a trunk fo curioufly wrought and to have fo much riches expofed to the indifcretion or knavery of a lockfmith,

that

that might talk publicly of them, and by that means inform all robbers of it. ' What ufe are thefe favours ' of, (Fortunio cried) fince I can neither enjoy them ' myfelf nor let my father receive any benefit from ' them? Then mufing and walking about, he remembered he fhould confult his horfe: away he goes to the ftable, and whifpered foftly to him, ' Pray, Comrade, ' tell me where I fhall find the key of the Turkey-lea-' ther trunk.' ' In my ear,' (anfwered he.) The knight looked in his ear and faw a green ribbon, by which he pulled out the key. He opened the trunk, and filled three little chefts full of diamonds and piftoles, one for his father, and two for his fifters, and fent the governor's man with them, defiring him not to ftop night nor day, till he arrived at the old count's. When the meffenger told him he came from his fon the knight, and brought him a very heavy cheft; he was very much furprifed at what it could contain, for he knew he had fo little money when he fet out, that he could not buy any thing, nor pay the perfon for bringing his prefent. Firft he opened his letter, and when he faw what his dear daughter had fent him, he was ready to die with joy: the fight of the jewels and gold, made good her words: but what was moft extraordinary, when the two fifters opened their chefts, there were nought but cut glafs and falfe piftoles; fo unwilling was the fairy that they fhould receive any favours from her: infomuch that they thought their fifter mocked them, and thereupon conceived an inexpreffible hatred againft her. The count feeing them fo angry, gave them a great many of the jewels; but as foon as ever they touched them, they changed like the reft, by which they knew fome unknown power acted againft them, and begged of their father to keep them to himfelf.

Fortunio never ftaid for the return of the meffenger, fo fhort was the time limited to obey the king's edict in, but went and took his leave of the governor. The whole city was affembling together to fee him: his perfon and all his actions had fomewhat fo engaging in them, that they could not but love and admire him.

He .

He never fpoke, but they expreffed a pleafure at every word; and the crowd was fo great, that he who had been ufed all his life-time to the country, knew not what it was owing to. After all civilities paid and received, he fet forward on his journey, and was entertained moft agreeably by his horfe, who told him of a great many remarkable things both in old and modern hiftories, until they arrived at a vaft foreft; when Comrade faid to the knight, ' Mafter, there lives her a man ' who may be of great ufe to us: he is a wood-man, ' and one who is gifted.' ' What do you mean by that?' (interrupted the knight.) ' One (faid the horfe) who is ' endowed by fairies with fome rare qualities; there- ' fore we muft engage him to go along with us.' At that inftant they came to the place where the wood-man was at work. The young knight approached him with a fweet and pleafant air, and afked him feveral queftions about the place where they were: whether there were any wild beafts in the foreft, and if people were allowed to hunt them; to which the woodman returned him very fuitable anfwers. Then he afked him who helped him to fell fo many trees; he anfwered, he had felled them all himfelf; and that it was the work only of fome few hours; and that he muft fell a few more to make a little burden. ' What (faid the knight) do you pretend to carry all this wood to day.' ' O Sir, ' (faid ftrong-back, which was his name) I am extra- ' ordinary ftrong.' ' Then (faid fortunio) your gain ' muft be great.' ' Very little, (replied the woodman) ' we are very poor in this place; and every one does ' his own work.' ' Since it is fo (added the knight) ' come along with me, and you fhall want nothing; ' and when you have a mind to go home again, I will ' give you money to defray your expences.' Which propofal he approved of, and left his wedges and other tools, and followed his new mafter.

When he had croffed the foreft, he faw a man in the plain, holding in his hands ribbons, with which he tied his legs, leaving one would think or imagine, fcarce liberty enough to walk. Comrade ftopped, and faid to

his

his mafter, ' This is another gifted man; you will
' have occafion for him, therefore take him along with
' you.' At that the fortunate knight advanced towards
him with his natural gracefulnefs, and afked him
why he tied his legs fo? ' O, (anfwered he) I am pre-
' pairing for a hunt.' ' How (faid the knight, fmiling)
' do you pretend to run beft when you are fettered?'
' No, Sir, (replied he) I do not pretend to run fo faft,
' but that is not my intention; there are neither ftags
' nor hares, but what I out-run when my legs are at
' liberty; fo that by always out-going them they efcape,
' and I feldom catch them.' ' You feem to me a very
' extraordinary man, (faid the knight) what is your
' name?' ' Lightfoot (replied he) and I am very well
' known in this country.' ' If you would fee another,
' (added our hero) I fhould be glad you would go with
' me: I will ufe you very kindly.' Which offer, Lightfoot, as he lived but indifferently, accepted of with
thanks, and followed the fortunate knight.

The next day he met with a man by a marfh fide,
binding his eyes. The horfe faid to his mafter, ' I
' would advife you, Sir, to take this man into your fer-
' vice.' Fortunio afked him what made him bind his
eyes; to which he anfwered, that he faw too clearly;
that he could fee game above four leagues; and that
he never fhot but he killed always more than he defired;
that he was forced to bind his eyes, left he fhould deftroy
all the partridges, pheafants, &c. in the country. ' You
' are a notable man, (replied Fortunio) what is your
' name?' ' They call me Markfman, (anfwered he)
' and I would not leave off that employ for any thing
' in the world.' ' However, (faid the knig t) I have
' a great defire to propofe to you to travel along with
' me; it fhall not hinder you from exercifing your
' talent.' The Markfman raifed fome objections, and
the knight found it harder to get his confent than any
of the reft; for thefe fort of people are generally
great lovers of liberty: however he brought it about,
and they all left the marfh together.

After

(

After some days journey they came by a long meadow, where they saw a man laid all on one side upon the ground. 'Master (said Comrade) this is a gifted 'man, who will, I foresee, be very necessary to you.' Fortunio went into the meadow, and desired to know 'what he was doing. 'I want some simples (answered 'he) and I am listening to the grass that is growing, 'to know if there are any such as I want coming up.' 'What (said the knight) is your ear so quick as to hear 'the grass grow, and know what will come up?' 'Yes, '(replied he) and for that reason I am called Fine-Ear.' 'Well, Fine-Ear, (said Fortunio) have you an incli- 'nation to follow me? I will give you good wages; 'you shall have no reason to complain.' This pro- posal was so agreeable to him, he, without any manner of hesitation, added himself to increase their number.

The knight pursuing his travels, saw by a great road side a man whose cheeks were so blown up, that he re- presented the picture of Eolus; he was standing with his face towards a high hill, about two leagues off, on which there stood fifty or sixty windmills. The horse said to his master, 'There is another of our gifted men; do 'what you can to take him along with you.' Fortunio, who was as engaging in his person as speech, accosted him, asked him, what he was doing there. 'I am blowing 'a little, Sir, (answered he) to set those mills at work.' 'You seem too far off,' (said the knight.) 'On the 'contrary (replied the blower) I am too nigh; if I did 'not hold in my breath, I should overturn the mills, 'and perhaps the hill itself; so that by this means I 'often do a great deal of mischief against my will. I 'will tell you, Sir, I once was in love, and very ill used 'by my mistress, and as I sighed in the woods, my sighs 'tore up trees by their roots and made such a havock, 'that in this country they called me the Boisterer.' 'If 'you are troublesome to them (said Fortunio) go along 'with me; here are those that will bear you company, 'who have each of them extraordinary talents.' 'I 'have a natural curiosity (replied the Boisterer) and 'on that condition accept of your offer.'

Every

Every thing fucceeding thus to Fortunio's defire, he
left this place, and after croffing a thick inclofed country,
faw a large lake into which feveral fprings difcharged
their waters; and by its fide a man who looked very
earneftly at him. ‘ Sir (faid Comrade to his mafter)
‘ this man is wanting to compleat your equipage; it
‘ would be well if you could engage him to follow you.’
The knight went to him and faid, ‘ Pray, friend, what
‘ are you doing there?’ ‘ You fhallfee, Sir, (anfwered
‘ the man) as foon as the lake is full, I will drink it up
at one draught; for I am very dry, though I have
‘ emptied it twice already.’ Accordingly he ftooped
down, and left fcarce enough for the leaft fifh to fwim
in. Fortunio and his troop were all very much furprifed. ‘ What, (faid he) are you always thus thirfty?’
‘ No, (faid the water-drinker) only after eating falt
‘ meat, or upon a wager. I am known by the name of
‘ Tippler.’ ‘ Come along with me, Tippler, (faid the
‘ knight) and you fhall tipple wine, you will like better
‘ than this water.’ This promife carried too great a
temptation with it for Tippler to withftand, who immediately got up, and followed them.

The knight had got within fight of the place of ren-
dezvous, where they were all to affemble, when he perceived a man who eat fo greedily, that though he had
fixty thoufand loves of bread before him, he feemed refolved not to leave one bit. Comrade faid to his mafter,
‘ Sir, you only want this man; pray engage him to go
‘ with you.’ Upon which the knight made up to him,
and fmiling faid, ‘ Are you refolved to eat up all this
‘ bread at your breakfaft?’ ‘ Yes (replied he) and am
‘ vexed to fee fo little: thefe bakers are a lazy fort of
‘ people, who care not if one was ftarved.’ ‘ If you
‘ eat as much every day (added Fortunio) you are
‘ able to caufe a famine in the country of the world.’
‘ O! Sir, (repled Grugeon, which was his name, and
‘ which fignifies a great eater) I fhould be forry to have
‘ fo great a ftomach, fince neither what I could get my-
‘ felf, nor what my neighbours had, would fatisfy me:
‘ indeed, fometimes I am glad to regale myfelf after

3   ‘ this

' this manner.' ' Well, Grugeon (said the knight) if
' you will follow me, you shall not want for good cheer,
' nor repent your chusing me for your master.' Comrade, whose sense and foresight were of great service to
our knight, told him, it would be proper that he forbid
his attendants from boasting of their extraordinary gifts;
which he failed not to do and each of them swore they
would punctually obey his commands. Soon after the
knight, whose beauty and good mien far exceeded the
richness of his habit, entered the capital city, mounted
on his excellent horse, and followed by his seven attendants, for whom he provided rich liveries, laced with
gold, and good horses; and going to the best inn, stayed
there till the day appointed for the review; all which
time he was the subject of discourse of the whole city,
insomuch that the king hearing of him, had a great desire
to see him.

The troop assembled on a large plain, the king and
his sister, the queen dowager, came to review them.
She abated in no wise her pomp and state, notwithstanding the troubles of the kingdom; but dazzled Fortunio's
eyes with the riches with which she was adorned; whose
beauty had the same effect upon that noble train, as her
magnificence had on him. Every body inquired who
that handsome young knight was; and the king himself,
as he passed by, made a sign for him to come to him.
Fortunio alighted from off his horse, to make the king a
low bow, but at the same time could not forbear blushing,
seeing him look so earnestly at him, which gave a great
lustre to his complexion. ' I should be glad (said the
' king) to know who you are, and your name;' ' Sir,
' (answered he) I am called Fortunio, though I have
' no reason to bear that name, since my father is an old
' count who lives on the frontiers; who, though he is a
' man of birth, has no estate.' ' Though fortune may
' have proved unkind hitherto, (answered the king)
' she has made amends, by bringing you hither. I have
' a particular affection for you, and remember that
' your father did mine some signal services, which I will
' recompense in you.' ' It is just you should, (said
' the

' the queen dowager, who had not yet opened her lips)
' And as I am older than you, brother, I remember
' more particularly than you do, what great things the
' old count performed in the service of his country;
' therefore I desire I may have the care of the preferment
' of this young knight.'

Fortunio, overjoyed at this reception, could not thank
the king and queen enough, and durst not enlarge too
much on the sentiments of his acknowledgment, thinking it more respectful to hold his tongue, than to speak too
much, though what he did say was so proper and well adapt-
ed, that every one commended him. Afterwards he mounted his horse again, and mixed among the lords and gentlemen who attended on the king; when the queen calling him, often asked him questions, and turning herself
towards Florida, who was her confident, said to her softly, ' What do you think of this young spark? can
' there be a more noble air, and more regular features?
' I must confess, I never in my life saw any thing
' more lovely.'   Florida's sentiments differed not from
her mistress's; she praised him even to exaggeration.
Our knight could not forbear casting his eyes often on
the king, who was not only a handsome prince, but in
all his ways was engaging; and our female warrior,
though she had changed her habit, had not renounced
her sex, but was sensible of his merit.   The king told
Fortunio after the review, that he was afraid the war
would be very bloody, therefore he was resolved always
to keep him nigh his own person.   The queen dowager,
who was then by, said, she was just thinking that he
ought not to be exposed to the dangers of a long campaign,
and that as the place of the steward of her houshold was
vacant, she would give it to him.   ' No, (said the king)
' I will make him master of the horse to myself.'   Thus
they disputed who should prefer Fortunio; when the
queen, fearing lest she should too much betray the secret
emotions of her heart, yielded to the king.

There was never a day passed but Fortunio called for
his turkey-leather trunk, and took a new dress; by which
means he appeared more magnificent than all the princes

ces of the court: infömuch that the queen afked him often
how his father could afford to be at fo vaft an expence?
Sometimes fhe bantered him, and faid, ' Come, con-
' fefs truly, you have a miftrefs, who fupports you in
' all this finery.' Upon which Fortunio would blufh,
and excufe himfelf the beft he could. He acquitted himfelf admirably well in his poft, and his heart, which was
fenfible of a tendernefs for the king, attached him more
to his perfon than he wifhed to be. ' What is my fate,
' (faid our knight) I love a great and powerful king,
' without any hopes of the like return, or that he fhould
' have any regard for the pains I endure?' The king
' loaded him with his favours; he thought nothing well
done, but what was done by the handfome knight, and
the queen, deceived by his habit, thought ferioufly of
marrying him; but the inequality of their birth was the
' only obftacle that ftood in her way. Neither was fhe
the only perfon that was taken with the beautiful Fortunio, all the fine ladies of the court fighed for him.
He was continually peftered with tender letters, appoint-
ments for rendezvoufes, prefents, and a thoufand other
gallantries; which he anfwered with all imaginable indifference, which made them fufpect he had left a miftrefs behind him in his own country. At all tournaments he won the prize, and in hunting, or any other
fport, killed more game than all the company befides,
and danced at all balls more gracefully than all the
courtiers; in fhort, he charmed all who faw or heard
him.

The queen, that fhe might not be obliged to declare
her fentiments to him herfelf, charged Florida, to let
him underftand, that fuch marks of bounty from a young
queen ought not to be fo carelefsly received. Florida,
who had not been able to avoid the fate of moft that
had feen this knight, was very much embarraffed with
this commiffion; he appeared too lovely in her eyes, for
her to think of preferring her miftrefs's intereft before
her own; infomuch that whenever the queen gave her
an opportunity of difcourfing with him, inftead of
fpeaking of the beauty and great qualifications of that

B   princefs,

princefs, fhe told him how ill-humoured fhe was, how much her woman endured with her; how unjuft fhe was, and the ill ufe fhe made of the great power fhe had ufurped; and at laft, comparing fentiments, faid, ' Though I was not born to be a queen, I ought to have ' been one, fince I have a great and generous foul, that ' induces me to do good to every body. O! (continued ' fhe) was I in that high ftation, how happy would I ' make the charming Fortunio! he fhould love me out ' of gratitude, if he could not love me through inclina- ' tion.'

The young knight was entirely at a lofs, and knew not what anfwer to make, but ever after carefully avoid- ed having any private difcourfe with her; while the im- patient queen never failed to afk Florida how far fhe had wrought on Fortunio, who faid to her, ' He is, Ma- ' dam, fo timorous, that he will not believe any thing ' that I tell him favourably from you, or pretends not ' to believe it, becaufe he is engaged in fome other paf- ' fion.' ' I believe fo too, (faid the alarmed queen) ' but is it poffible his love fhould hold out againft his ambition?' ' And can you, Madam (replied Florida) ' bear the thoughts of owing his heart to your crown? ' ought a princefs fo young and beautiful as you are, ' to have recourfe to a diadem?' ' Yes, to every thing, ' (cried the queen) when it is to fubdue a rebellious ' heart.' By this Florida knew very well that it was impoffible to cure her miftrefs of her paffion. The queen waited every day for fome happy effect from the cares of her confident; but the fmall progrefs fhe made on Fortunio, obliged her to find out other ways to dif- courfe with him. As fhe knew that he went early every morning into a little wood, into which the windows of her apartment looked; fhe arofe with the morning, and looking out fhe perceived him walking in a carelefs melancholy air, and calling Florida, faid to her, ' What ' you told me appears but too true; Fortunio, without ' difpute, is in love with fome lady, either in this ' court, or in his own country: obferve but the fadnefs ' which hangs on his face.' ' I have taken notice of it in
' all

‘ all the converfation I had with him (replied Florida)
‘ therefore, Madam, it would be well if you could for-
‘ get him.’ ‘ It is now too late, (cried the queen,
‘ fetching a deep figh) but if he goes into that green
‘ arbour, we will go to him.’   Florida durft in no wife
offer to oppofe the queen, though fhe had a great defire
to it; for fhe was cruelly afraid fhe fhould be loved by
Fortunio, knowing a rival of her rank to be always dangerous.   When the queen came within fome fmall diftance of the arbour, fhe heard the knight, whofe voice
was very agreeable, fing thefe words:

In vain foft eafe, the love tofs'd heart purfues;
Ev'n in poffeffion of the long fought joy,
We rob the bounteous God of half his dues,
And future fears the prefent blifs deftroy.

Fortunio made thefe lines, with relation to the fentiment wherewith the young king had infpired her, the
favours fhe had received from that prince, and the ap-
prehenfions fhe was under, left fhe fhould be known,
and be forced to leave a court, which fhe chofe to live in
fooner than any other place in the world. The queen
who ftopped to hear her, was in cruel uneafinefs: ‘ What
‘ am I going to attempt? (faid fhe foftly to Florida)
‘ this young ingrate defpifes the honour of pleafing me,
‘ thinks himfelf happy, feems content with his conqueft,
‘ and facrifices me to another.’ ‘ He is now at that age
‘ (anfwered Florida) when reafon has not fully eftablifh-
‘ ed itfelf. If I durft give your majefty advice, it
‘ fhould be to forget him, fince he knows not how to va-
‘ lue his good fortune.’ The queen, who would have
been better pleafed that her confident had fpoke after
another manner, caft an angry eye upon her, and advancing forwards, went directly into the arbour where
the knight was and pretended to be furprifed to find
him there, and to be vexed he fhould fee her in a difha-
bille, though at the fame time fhe had neglected nothing
that was rich and gallant. As foon as he faw her, he
was for retiring, out of refpect; but fhe bid him ftay,
that

that she might lean on him back again, ' I was this
' morning (said she) agreeably awakened by the warb-
' ling of the birds, and the freshness of the air invited
' me to come nigher to them. Alas! how happy are
' they! they know nought but pleasures, they know no
' troubles.' I am of opinion, madam (replied Fortu-
' nio) that they are not absolutely exempt from trou-
' bles and disquiets! they are always in danger of the
' murdering shot and snares of sportsmen, besides that
' of the birds of prey, which make a cruel war upon
' them; and then again, when a hard and severe win-
' ter congeals the earth, and covers it with snow, they
' die for want of food, and are every year put to the
' trouble of seeking out a new mistress.' ' Do you
' think it then a trouble? (said the queen smiling)
' there are men who do it every month. What (con-
' tinued she) you seem surprised, as if your heart was
' not of this stamp, and that you have not hitherto been
' given to change.' ' I cannot yet tell Madam, (said he)
' what I may be capable of, since I was never sensible
' of love; but I dare believe, if I should be, my passion
' would be lasting.' ' You have never been in love!
' (cried the queen, looking so earnest at him, that the
' poor knight blushed) you have not been in love? O
' Fortunio! how can you tell a queen so? who reads, in
' your face and eyes, the passion that possesses your
' heart, and which your own words, which you sung to
' a new fashioned tune, have informed me of.' ' In-
' deed, Madam (answered the knight) the lines were
' made, but I made them without any particular design;
' for my companions and acquaintances engage me to
' make drinking catches, (though I drink naught but
' water) and tender passionate songs; so that I sing
' both love and bacchus, though I am neither a lover
' nor a drinker.'

The queen listened to him with that concern, that
she could hardly contain herself. What he said, re-
kindled in her heart the hope Florida would have ba-
nished: ' If I could think you sincere, (said she) I should
' have reason to be surprised, that you have not found

' in

' in this court a lady amiable enough to fix your choice.'
' Madam (replied Fortunio) I have fo much to do in
' the office I am in, I have no time to throw away in
' fighing.' ' Then you love nothing?' (added fhe with
' eagernefs.) ' No, Madam (faid he) I have not a
' heart of fo gallant a character; I am a kind of mifan-
' thropift, that loves my liberty, and would not lofe it
' for all the world.' The queen fat herfelf down, and
fixing her eyes moft obligingly on him, replied, ' There
' are fome chains fo eafy and glorious to bear, that if
' fortune has deftined any fuch for you, I would ad-
' vife you to renounce your liberty.' In this difcourfe
her eyes explained her thoughts but two intelligibly for
our knight, whofe fufpicions were too great before not
to be confirmed in them; and fearing left the converfation fhould go too far, he pulled out a watch, and fet-
ting the hand forward, faid, ' I beg of your majefty
' to give me leave to go to the palace, it is the king's
' time of rifing, and he ordered me to be at his levee.'
' Go, indifferent youth, (faid fhe, fetching a deep figh)
' you are in the right to pay court to my brother; but
' remember it would not be amifs to let me have fome
' fhare of your devoirs.' The queen followed him with
her eyes; then lowering them, and reflecting on what
had paffed, blufhed with fhame and rage; and what
troubled her moft, was, Florida's being a witnefs, and
the joyful air that appeared all over her countenance,
which was as much as to fay, fhe had better have taken
her advice, than fpoke to Fortunio.

Florida acted her part very well with the queen, and
comforted her the beft fhe could, giving her fome flattering hopes, of which at that time fhe ftood in great need.
' Fortunio, Madam, (faid fhe) thinks himfelf fo much
' beneath you, that perhaps he did not underftand what
' you meant, and I think he has affured you he loves
' no perfon.' As it is natural for us to flatter ourfelves,
the queen recovered fomewhat out of her fears, not dream-
ing in the leaft that the malicious Florida was engaging
her to declare herfelf more plainly, that he might offend
her the more by the indifference of his anfwers. The

knight

knight, for his part, was in the utmoft confufion, the
fituation he was in feemed cruel, and he would have
made no difficulty to have left the court, had not the
fatal ftroke, wherewith the little god had wounded his
heart, detained him in fpite of himfelf. He never came
near the queen but on drawing-room nights, and then
with the king; and as foon as fhe perceived this new
change in his behaviour, fhe gave him often the moft
favourable opportunities to make his court to her, which
he as often neglected; when one day, as fhe was going
down fome fteps into the gardens, fhe faw him croffing
a large alley, and making towards the woods. Upon
which, calling to him, he, left fhe fhould be difpleafed,
came to her and pretened that he did not fee her.
' You remember knight (faid fhe) the converfation we
' had fome time fince in the green arbour.' ' I am not,
' Madam, (anfwered he) capable of forgetting that
' honour.' ' Then, without doubt, (faid fhe) the
' queftions I put to you were not very pleafing; for
' fince that day, you would not let it be in my power
' to afk you any more.' ' As chance alone, (anfwered
' he) procured me that favour, I thought it would be
' too great boldnefs to pretend to any other.' ' Say
' rather ungrateful man, (continued fhe blufhing) you
' have avoided my prefence: you know my fentiments
' but too well.' Fortunio, through modefty and confufion, lowered his eyes, and as he did not make a quick
reply, ' You are very much confounded, (faid fhe) go,
' feek not for an anfwer, I underftand you better than
' I would.' She had, perhaps, faid a great deal more,
but that fhe perceived the king coming that way; whereupon fhe made towards him, feeing him penfive and
melancholy, conjured him to tell her the reafon, ' You
' know, (faid the king) that I have received advice
' this month of a dragon of a prodigious fize, that ra-
' vages the whole country. I thought he might be killed,
' and to that end gave neceffary orders; but all that has
' been tried has proved in vain. He devours my fub-
' jects and their flocks, and all that comes nigh him; he
' poifons all the rivers and lakes he drinks at, and
                                         ' wherever

' wherever he lies, withers all the grass and herbs about him.'

While the king was making this complaint, the enraged queen was thinking how she might sacrifice the knight to her resentment. ' I am not unacquainted with ' the ill news you have received; Fortunio, whom you ' saw with me, informed me thereof; but, brother, ' you will be surprised at what I have to tell you; he has ' begged of me with the greatest importunity, to ask ' your leave to let him go to fight this terrible dragon ; ' indeed he has a wonderful address and handles his ' arms so well, that I am not so much amazed at his ' presuming so much of himself; besides, he has told ' me he has a secret, by which he can lay the most wake- ' ful dragon asleep: but that must not be mentioned, ' because it shews not so much courage in the action.' ' Be it how it will, (replied the king) it will be glo- ' rious for him, and of great service to us, if he should ' succeed; but I am afraid this proceeds from an in- ' discreet zeal, and that it should cost him his life.' ' No, brother (added the queen) fear not, he has told ' me very surprising things on this subject. You know ' he is naturally very severe; and besides, what honour ' can he hope to gain by throwing away his life rashly ? ' In short, (continued she) I have promised to obtain ' for him what he so earnestly desires, and if you refuse ' him, you will break his heart.' ' I consent (said the ' king) yet I must own, not very freely: however, let us ' call him ' And thereupon making a sign for him to come to him, said to him in an obliging manner, ' I un- ' derstand by the queen, you have a great desire to fight ' the dragon, that preys so much on our country ; which ' is so bold a resolution, that I can scarcely belive you ' know the danger you run.' ' I have represented that ' already to him, (answered the queen) but his zeal for ' your service, and his desire to signalize himself, are so ' great, that nothing can dissuade him from it; and ' therefore I foresee some happy success will attend him.'

Fortunio was very much surprised to hear the king and queen talk after this manner, and had too much

fenfe

fenfe not to penetrate into the ill defigns of that princefs; but his fweetnefs of temper would not fuffer him
to explain himfelf. So, without returning any anfwer,
he let her talk on, while he made low bows; which the
king took for fo many new entreaties to grant what he
fo much defired. ' Go, (faid the king, fighing) go
' where honour calls; I know you do every thing fo well,
' and in particular have fo much courage and conduct,
' that this monfter will not be able to efcape your arms.'
' Sir, (anfwered the knight) however fortune decides
' the fight, I fhall be fatisfied: fince I fhall either deli-
' ver you from a terrible fcourge, or die in your fervice:
' But honour me with one favour, which will be infinitely
' dear to me.' ' Afk what you will have,' (faid the
' king.) ' Then let me be fo bold (continued he) as to
' beg your picture.' The king was mightily pleafed,
that he fhould think of his picture at a time when his
thoughts might have been employed on fo many other
important things, and the queen was chagrined anew,
that he had not made the fame requeft to her. The king
returned to his palace, and the queen to hers, and Fortunio, who was not a little embarraffed on his word which
he had given, went to his horfe: ' Comrade (faid he)
' I have ftrange news to tell your.' ' I know it, Sir,
' already,' (replied the horfe) ' What fhall we then do?'
(afked Fortunio) ' We muft go as foon as poffible;
' (anfwered the horfe) get the king's commiffion, where-
' by he orders you to fight the dragon, and afterwards
' we will do our duty.' Thefe words were very com-
fortable to our young knight, who failed not to wait on
the king early the next morning in a campaining habit,
as handfome and gallant as any of his other.

As foon as the king faw him, he cried out, ' What,
' are you ready to go?' ' Yes, Sir, (replied he) one
' cannot make too much hafte to execute your com-
' mands; therefore I am come to take my leave of you.'
The king could not but relent, feeing fo young, fo beautiful, and fo accomplifhed a knight, then going to expofe himfelf to the greateft danger, man could ever en-
counter; he embraced him, and gave him his picture fet in
diamonds,

diamonds, which Fortunio received with extraordinary joy; for the king's great qualities had such an effect upon him, that he could not think any so lovely as him; and if he had any reluctancy to go, it proceeded more from being deprived of his presence, than his fear of being devoured by the dragon. The king would have a general order included in Fortunio's commission, for all his subjects to aid and assist him, whenever he should stand in need. Afterwards he took his leave of the king, and that nothing might be remarked in his behaviour, went also to the queen, who was set at her toilet, surrounded by a great number of ladies. She changed colour, as soon as ever she saw him, so much had she to reproach herself withal; he saluted her respectfully, and asked her if she would honour him with her commands, since he was just then going. These last words put her into the utmost consternation, while Florida, who knew not what the queen had plotted against the knight, remained like one thunder-struck, and would willingly have had some private discourse with him, but that he avoided it as much as possible: ' I beseech Heaven (said ' the queen) that you may conquer, and return in ' triumph.' ' Madam, (replied the knight) your ma ' jesty honours me too much, and I am sensible, knows ' very well the danger to which I shall be exposed; yet ' I have a great deal of confidence, and perhaps am the ' only person that entertains any hopes on this occasion.' The queen understood very well what he meant, and, without dispute, had returned him some answer to this reproach, had there not been so many witnesses present.

The king afterwards went away, and he ordered his seven notable domestics to take horse, and follow him, because the time was then come to make proof of what they could do. They all expressed their joy to serve him; and got every thing done in less than an hour's time, and went along with him, assuring him, that they would neglect nothing they could do to serve him; and when they were out in the country, shewed their address. Trinquet drank up the lake and ponds, and catched delicate fish for his master's dinner: Lightfoot hunted down ve-

nison

nifon, and catched hares by the ears; and for the good
Markfman, he neither gave partridge nor pheafant any
quarter; and whatever came they killed, Strongback
carried it. By this means Fortunio had no occafion to
draw his purfe-ftrings all his journey, and might have
had very good diverfion, if his thoughts had been lefs
employed on thofe he left behind him. The king's merit was always in his mind, and the queen's malice appeared fo great, that he could not but deteft her. Thus
he travelled all the way very thoughtful, till he was
roufed from his mufings by the fhrieks of poor peafants
half devoured by the dragon. Some that had efcaped,
he faw flying as faft as they could, who would not ftop
nor ftay, which obliged him to ride after them to get in-
telligence. After he had talked with them, and learnt
that the dragon was not far off, he afked them how
they fecured themfelves from him. To which they
anfwered, ' That as water was very fcarce in that coun-
' try, that they had none but what they preferved when it
' rained in ponds; at which the dragon, when he went
' his rounds came to drink, making a terrible noife and
' roaring, which might be heard a league off; that every
' body hid themfelves, and fhut their doors and windows.'

The knight went into an inn, not fo much to reft himfelf, as to advife with his horfe; When every one was
retired and gone to reft, he went into the ftable, and
faid, ' Comrade, how fhall we conquer this dragon?'
To which the horfe replied, ' Sir, I will dream to night,
' and give you an account in the morning; when he came
again, he faid, ' Let Fine-Fear liften whether the dra-
' gon is nigh at hand, or not.' Fine-Ear laid himfelf
on the ground, and heard the dragon about feven leagues
off. When the horfe was informed of this, he faid to
Fortunio, ' Bid Trinquit go and drink up all the water
' out of a large pond, and Strongback carry wine enough
' to fill it: then let there be dried raifins prepared,
' and falted meats fet by it: afterwards order all the
' inhabitants to keep their houfes, and likewife do you
' and your attendants the fame; the dragon will not
' fail to eat and drink, he will like the wine, and you
                                                      will

THE STORY OF FORTUNIO.

The STORY OF FORTUNIO.

' will fee what will happen.' No fooner had the horfe
thus appointed what was to be done, but every one did
what he was ordered: the knight went to a houfe, whence
he might fee the pond; and was no fooner within the
doors but the dragon came and drank a little: afterwards
he eat fome of that repaft prepared for him; and then
drank fo much, that he was quite drunk, infomuch that
he could not ftir. He was laid on one fide, with his
head hanging down, and his eyes fhut. When Fortunio
faw him in this condition, he thought proper to lofe no
time, but went out with his fword in his hand, and attacked him. The dragon finding himfelf wounded on
all fides, would have got up, and fallen upon the knight,
who overjoyed that he had reduced him to this extremity,
called his attendants to bind this monfter, that the king
might have the honour and pleafure of putting an end to
his life, and that being fo bound, he might be carried
without danger, to the capital city.

Fortunio marched at the head of his little troop, and
when he was within fome few hours march of the palace,
he fent Lightfoot to acquaint the king with the good news
of his fuccefs; which feemed almoft incredible, till the
monfter appeared bound faft upon a machine for that
purpofe. The king went to Fortunio, embraced him,
and faid, ' The Gods have referved this victory for you.
' I am not fenfible of half fo much joy to fee this mon-
' fter in this condition, as to fee my dear knight again.'
' Sir (replied he) your majefty yourfelf may give him
' the laft blow, I brought him hither on purpofe that he
' might receive it at your hand.' At that the king drew
his fword, and killed this his moft cruel enemy, while all
the people gave fhouts and acclemations of joy at fuccefs
little expected. Florida, who during his abfence, had
not enjoyed many quiet hours, was not long before fhe
was informed of her charming knight's return, and ran
to tell the queen; who was fo much furprifed and confounded through love and hatred, that fhe could return
no anfwer to what her favourite told her, but reproached
herfelf a thoufand times for the ill turn fhe had played
him; but then again would have been better pleafed to

have

have heard of his death, than to fee him fo indifferent: infomuch that fhe knew not whether fhe fhould be vexed or pleafed at his return to court, where his prefence might difturb her repofe. The king, impatient to tell her the happy fuccefs of fo extraordinary an adventure, went into her chamber, leaning on the knight. ' Here ' is the man (faid he) that has vanquifhed the dragon, ' and has done me the greateft fervice I could defire ' from the moft faithful fubject. It was to you madam, ' that he firft fpoke of his defire to fight that monfter, ' and I hope you will refpect him for the danger to ' which he expofed himfelf.' The queen compofing her countenance, honoured Fortunio with a gracious re-ception, and a thoufand praifes, found him much more lovely than when he went away, and gave him to under-ftand how much her heart was wounded, by looking fo earneftly at him.

But not fatisfied with explaining her fentiments by her eyes, one day as fhe was hunting with the king, fhe pretended to be out of order, that fhe could not fol-low the dogs: and turning herfelf towards the young knight. who was juft by her, faid to him, ' You will do ' me the pleafure to ftay with me, for I have a mind ' to alight, and reft myfelf a little.' Then bidding thofe who attended on her to go forwards, fhe and For-tunio alighted, and fat down by a brook-fide, where fhe remained for fome time in a profound filence, thinking on what fhe fhould fay. Afterwards lifting up her eyes, and fixing them on the knight, fhe faid, ' As good in-' tentions do not always fhew themfelves, I am afraid ' you have not penetrated into the motives that engaged ' me to prefs the king to fend you to fight the dragon. ' I was affured by a fore knowledge, that never deceives ' me, that you would behave yourfelf with bravery, of ' which your enemies fpoke very indifferently, becaufe ' you went not to the army, that you lay under a ne-' ceffity of performing fome fuch illuftrious action ' as this to ftop their mouths. I fhould have acquainted ' you (continued fhe) with what they faid on this fub-' ject, or ought to have done it, but that I was perfuad-
' ed

' ed your refentment would be attended with fome
' fatal confequences, and that it would be better to
' filence your enemies by your intrepidity in danger,
' than by an authority that would fhew more of the
' favourite than the foldier.' ' The diftance between
' us is fo great, madam (replied he modeftly) that I am
' not worthy of this explanation, nor the care you took
' to hazard my life for the fake of my honour. Heaven
' has protected me more than my enemies wifhed for,
' and I fhall efteem myfelf always happy to venture for
' the king, and your fervice, a life which is more indif-
' ferent to me than fome people imagine.'

This refpectful reproach embarraffed the queen, who
underftood very well what he meant; but fhe thought
him too amiable to exafperate him by too fevere a reply.
On the contrary fhe pretended to be of his opinion; and
told him again, how glorioufly he had flain the dragon.
Fortunio had been fo cautious, to let no perfon know that
it was owing to the affiftance of his retinue, but boafted
of his meeting that terrible enemy barefaced, and that
the victory was gained entirely by his courage. In the
mean time the queen, who thought not fo much on what
he was telling her, interrupted him, to afk him if he was
fatisfied how much fhe was interrefted in his fafety; and
that converfation had been carried farther, but he faid, .
' Madam, the king is coming this way, I hear the horn,
' and will not your majefty be pleafed to mount again?'
' No (faid fhe, with an air of rage) it is enough that
' you go.' ' The king, madam (replied he) will blame
' me for leaving you alone, in a place expofed to fo
' many dangers.' ' I difpenfe with this your care
' (added fhe in a haughty tone) Go, your prefence is
' troublefome.' At that the knight made a low bow,
mounted his horfe, and rid out of fight, very much concerned at the confequences that might attend this new
refentment. Upon this he confulted his horfe: ' Tell
' me, Comrade (faid he) whether this love-fick paffion-
' ate queen will find out another monfter for me?'
' No other befide herfelf (replied the horfe) but fhe is
' ftill more dangerous than the dragon you have killed,
                                                    and

' and will exercife both your patience and virtue fuffi-
' ciently.'   ' Will fhe make me lofe the king's favour
' (faid he) for that is all I am afraid of.'   ' I cannot
' tell what will happen in relation to that (faid Com-
' rade) it is enough that I am always upon the watch.'
There was no more faid then becaufe the king appeared,
and Fortunio went to him, and told him the queen was
indifpofed, and had ordered him to ftay with her,   ' I
' think (faid the king fmiling) you are very much in
' her favour, and declare your mind more freely to her
' than to me: I have not yet forgot your requeft, to
' her to procure you leave to fight the dragon.'   ' Sir,
' (anfwered the knight) I dare not pretend to clear myfelf
' from what you alledge againft me: But I can affure
' your majefty, I look upon your favour and the queen's
' with a great deal of difference; and was a fubject al-
' lowed to make his fovereign his confidant, I fhould
' do myfelf an infinite pleafure to declare to you the
' fentiments of my heart.'   Here the king interrupted
him, to afk where he had left the queen, who all the
time of their difcourfe was complaining to Florida of
Fortunio's indifference.   ' The fight of him (cried fhe)
' is hateful to me: either he or I muft leave the court,
' for I cannot bear that fuch an ungrateful wretch fhould
' fhew me fo much difdain; what man would not think
' himfelf happy to pleafe fo powerful a queen? He is
' the only perfon whom the Gods have referved to dif-
' turb the repofe of my life.'   Florida was in no wife
' difpleafed to fee her miftrefs fo chagrined, but inftead
of appeafing her, rather aggravated her, by recalling to
her remembrance a thoufand circumftances, which fhe
perhaps would not have taken notice of: which increafed
her rage, and made her think on a new project to ruin
the poor knight.

When the king came to her, he expreffed his concern
for her health; to which fhe faid, ' I muft own I was
' very ill, but one cannot be long fo, when Fortunio's
' by, he is fo merry, and his jefts are fo diverting: but
' you muft know, (continued fhe) he has defired me to
' afk another favour of your majefty. He infifts, with
' the

' the utmoft confidence, that he fhall fucceed in one o
' the moft rafh enterprizes imaginable.'　' What
' (cried the king) would he fight with fome new dra-
' gon?'　' With a great many at once (faid fhe) and
' makes as if he was fure to conquer. I will tell you;
' in fhort, he boafts to make the emperor reftore us to
' all our treafures, and to do it without an army.'
' What a pity is this (replied the king) that this poor
' boy fhould be guilty of fo much extravegance?'　' His
' victory over the dragon (added the queen) has puffed
' him up; and what do you hazard, in giving him
' leave to expofe himfelf again for your fervice?'　' I
' hazard his life, which is dear to me (replied the king)
' I fhould be very forry to be the occafion of his death.'
To this the queen anfwered, that his defire was fo great,
that if he refufed, he would languifh and die away.
The king upon this, looked very melancholy, and faid,
' I cannot imagine who it is that fills his head with thefe
' chimeras; it is unknown what I endure to fee him in
' this condition.'　' Why the matter is (replied the
' queen) he has fought a dragon, and been victorious,
' perhaps he may fucceed as well in this; I have often
' a very juft forefight, and my mind now tells me, that
' this undertaking will not be unfortunate; therefore,
' brother, oppofe not his zeal.'　' Let him be called
' then, (faid the king) and his dangers be reprefented
' to him.'　' That is the way to make him defpair,
' (replied the queen) he will believe you are againft his
' going; and I affure you he is not to be detained by
' any confideration that regards himfelf; for I faid all
' that can be thought on that fubject.'　' Well (cried
' the king) I confent.'　Upon this, the queen was overjoyed, and called Fortunio in: ' Go, knight (faid fhe)
' and thank the king; he has granted the leave you fo
' much defired, to go to the emperor Matapa, and make
' him, by fare means or force, reftore our treafures:
' make the fame difpatch, as when you went to fight
' the dragon.'
　Fortunio at firft was furprifed, but was foon fenfible
that this proceeded from the queen's rage; however he
　　　　　　　　　　　　　　　　　　　　　　　felt

felt a fecret pleafure, in being able to lay down his life for a prince that was fo dear to him: and without excufing himfelf from fuch an extraordinary commiffion, kneeled on one knee and kiffed the king's hand, whofe heart at that inftant relented. The queen felt an inward fhame, to fee with what refpect he behaved himfelf, though fent to meet a certain death. ‘ Would to heaven (faid fhe to herfelf) he had any regard for me; ‘ how noble it is not to contradict what I have advanced, ‘ but rather to bear the ill turn I have done him, than ‘ complain !’ The king faid little to the knight, but mounted his horfe again; and the queen pretended all that time to be ill went into her chaife. Fortunio accompanied them to the end of the foreft, and afterwards returned back to have fome difcourfe with his horfe: ‘ My faithful Comrade (faid he) 'tis done, I muft die, ‘ the queen has compleated that which I never expected ‘ from her.’ ‘ My lovely mafter (replied the horfe) ‘ fright not yourfelf, though I have not been prefent at ‘ what is paffed, I know all; the embafly is not fo ter-‘ rible as you imagine.’ ‘ You do not know (contin-‘ ued the knight) that this emperor is the moft paffion-‘ ate of all men; and that if I propofe that he reftore ‘ what he has taken from the king my mafter, he will ‘ return me no other anfwer, than order a ftone to be ‘ tied about my neck, that I may be thrown into a river.’ ‘ I am not uninformed of his violence; (faid Comrade) ‘ but that does not hinder you from taking your people ‘ along with you, and if we perifh, it fhall be one and ‘ all; but I hope for better fuccefs.’

The knight returned home fomewhat comforted, where he gave the neceffary orders, and afterwards went to receive his credentials. ‘ Tell the emperor (faid the ‘ king) that I remand back all my fubjects he has in ‘ flavery, all my foldiers that are prifoners, all my ‘ horfes and other goods and treafure.’ ‘ What ‘ muft I offer him for all this?’ (faid Fortunio.) ‘ No-‘ thing (anfwered the king) but my friendfhip.’ The young ambaffador had no occafion for a great memory to keep thefe inftructions in his mind; He went without

seeing

feeing the queen, at which fhe was very angry: but he had no reafon to regard that; for what could fhe do more in the height of her rage, than what fhe had accomplifhed in the greateft tranfport of friendfhip? and a tendernefs of this kind was to him the moft formidable thing in the world. Nay, her confidant, who knew the whole fecret, was enraged againft her miftrefs, for ftriving to facrifice the flower of all knighthood. Fortunio took whatever was neceffary for his journey out of his turkey-leather trunk, and was not content to cloath himfelf magnificently, but his feven fervants alfo: and as they had all excellent horfes, and Comrade feemed rather to fly than run, they arrived foon at the emperor's capital, which was no ways inferior to any city of Europe.

Fortunio was very much furprifed to fee a town of fuch a large extent. He demanded an audience of the emperor, and had it granted: but when he declared the fubject of his embaffy, though it was with a grace that gave force to his arguments, the emperor could not help fmiling. ‘ Were you at the head of five hundred thoufand men, (faid he) one might hearken to you; where- ‘ as, I am told you have only feven.’ ‘ I never under- ‘ took, Sir (faid Fortunio) to compel you by force of ‘ arms, but only by fome remonftrances.’ ‘ Whatever ‘ thofe be (added the emperor) you fhall never bring ‘ them to bear, unlefs you will do a thing that is juft ‘ now come into my head, that is, to find a man that ‘ can eat for his breakfaft as much hot bread as ferves ‘ this city for a whole day.’ The knight, at this propo- fition, feemed overjoyed, and as he fpoke not prefently, the emperor burft out into a laughter. ‘ Sir (faid For- ‘ tunio) I accept of your propofition, and will bring to- ‘ morrow a man, who fhall not only eat all the new ‘ bread, but alfo the ftale; order it to be brought out, ‘ and you fhall have the pleafure of feeing him lick up ‘ the very crumbs.’ The emperor faid he confented; and all the difcourfe of that day ran upon the folly of this ambaffador, whom Matapa fwore he would put to death, if he was not as good as his word. When he returned
back

back to the house where ambassadors were lodged, he
called Grugeon, and told him what had passed between
him and the emperor. ' Never be uneasy master (said
' Grugeon) I will eat till they be tired first.' However,
notwithstanding this assurance of Grugion's, Fortunio
could not help being under some apprehensions, but
forbid him from eating any supper, that he might eat
his breakfast the better.

A belcony was raised on purpose for the emperor,
and his consort and daughter, to see this fight. Fortunio came with his little train; and when he saw six great
mountains of bread, he turned pale; which had a quite
contrary effect upon Grugeon, he being pleased there-
with. The emperor laughed and jested with all his
court at the knight and his retinue's extravagant undertaking, while Grugeon was impatient for the signal.
At last it was made by the sounding of trumpets, and
beat of drum, and Grugeon fell upon one of the heaps,
and devoured it in less than a quarter of an hour, and
after that all the rest. Never was greater astonishment!
every body thought it was a piece of witchcraft, or that
their eyes deceived them: which made them go to the
place where the bread was piled up to be satisfied. Fortunio, who was infinitely well pleased with his good success, went to the emperor and asked him if he would be
as good as his word, to which the emperor, enraged to
be thus over-reached, replied, that it was too much to eat
without drinking; therefore he, or some of his train,
must drink all the water in the aqueducts and fountains
that were in that city, and all the wine in its cellars.
' Sir, (said Fortunio) you will put it out of my power
' to obey your commands; however, I will try, if I may
' flatter myself that you will restore to my master what
' I have demanded.' ' It shall be done, (said the em-
' peror) if you succeed in your undertaking.' The
knight asked the emperor, if he himself would be present; he answered, yes, he would, because so rare an
action deserved his curiosity: and getting that instant
into his chariot, carried him to a fountain of seven marble lions, which vomited up as much water as formed a
large

large river. Trinquit made up to the bafon, and without fo much as ever fetching his breath, drank it up, and
left the fifhes in the mud and fand. In like manner he
did by all the aqueducts and ponds belonging to the city.
After this experiment, the emperor never doubted but
he would drink the wine as well as the water: fo that he,
as well as the owners, had no inclination to try him:
but Trinquit complained highly of that injuftice, alleg-
ing that he had as much right to the wine as the water;
infomuch that the emperor, that he might not be thought
altogether covetous, confented to his defires. After that
Fortunio, taking his opportunity, put him in mind of
his promife; which he being unwilling to perform put
him out of humour. He called his council, and told
them how much he was concerned, that he had promifed this young ambaffador to return what he had taken
from his mafter; but withal, he thought the conditions
he agreed on were impracticable: therefore he affembled
them, to know how he might avoid what was fo much
againft his intereft and inclination. The princefs his
daughter, who was a very beautiful princefs, having
heard how much he was embarraffed, came to him, and
faid, ' Sir, as you know that none that ever ran with
' me, could ever boaft of the victory, if you think pro-
' per I will contend with him, and if he reaches firft the
' goal, you promife not to elude the word you have
' given.'
The emperor embraced his daughter, approved of
her propofal, and the next day, when Fortunio came to
an audience, faid to him, ' I have one thing more to
' inform you of, which is, that if you, or any of your at-
' tendants will run againft the princes, I fwear by all
' the elements, that if you or he gain the race, I will
' give your mafter all manner of fatisfaction. Fortunio
accepted the challenge, and Matapa appointed the time
to be within two hours, and accordingly fent to his daughter, to bid her prepare herfelf againft that time for the
exercife, which was what fhe had been ufed to from her
cradle. She appeared at the time in a long walk of
orange-trees above three miles long, which was fo carefully

fully rolled and managed, that there was not a ftone fo big as a pea to be feen. She was dreffed in a light gown of rofe-coloured taffety, embroidered in the feams with gold and filver; her hair, which was very fine, was tied behind her with a ribbon, and fell carelefsly on her fhoulders; her fhoes were made like pumps, without heels; fhe had on a girdle of jewels, to fhew her fhape, which was delicate: in fhort fhe thus appeared like another Atalanta. Soon after Fortunio followed, attended by Lighfoot and his other domeftics. The emperor and the whole court, were prefent, and feated along the walk, when the ambaffador propofed Lightfoot to have the honour to run with the princefs. He was furnifhed out of the miraculous trunk, with a fine white Holland habit, adorned with Flanders lace, filk ftockings of a fire-colour, with a white plume of feathers in his cap. In this drefs he appeared to have a good mien, but the princefs made no exceptions againft him; but before fhe fet out, fhe had liquor brought, to make her more fwift and ftrong. Our racer demanded the fame; the princefs faid, that it was too juft a requeft to be relufed, and ordered that he might have fome; but as he was not ufed to that liquor, which was very ftrong, it got into his head, and he lay down by an orange-tree, and fell faft afleep. In the mean time the fignal was given, and was repeated three times. The princefs waited fometime that lightfoot might awake and come to himfelf; but thinking it a matter of great confequence to free her father from his promife, fhe fet out with a charming grace and wonderful fwiftnefs.

Fortunio was at the other end of the walk, and knew nothing of what had happened, when he faw the princefs running by herfelf, and within half a mile of the goal. ‘ O ye powers! (cried he, fpeaking to his horfe) we are ‘ undone, I fee nothing of Lightfoot.’ ‘ Sir (faid Comrade) let Fine ear liften, he perhaps may inform you ‘ whereabouts he is.’ Thereupon Fine-ear laid himfelf down, and though he was three miles off, heard him fnore; whereupon he faid to them, he had no thoughts of coming, for that he was in as found a fleep as if he was in his bed.

‘ Alas!

' Alas! (cried Fortunio again) what shall we do?' ' O!
' (said Comrade) let the good Markfman let fly an
' arrow in the tip of his ear, to awake him.' At that
he took his bow immediately, and hit him fo nicely,
that the arrow went quite through his ear; the pain and
anguifh of which awakened him, and when he opened his
eyes, he faw the princefs almoft at the goal, and heard
great fhouts and acclamations of joy. At firft he was
furprifed, but he foon recovered what he had loft by
fleeping: he feemed as if he had been carried by the
wind and in fhort arrived firft at the goal, with the
arrow in his ear; for he had not time to pull it out.
The emperor was fo much amazed at the extraordinary
things that had happened fince the arrival of the ambaffador, that he believed the gods interrefted themfelves in
his behalf, and that be could no longer defer the per-
formance of his promife. He ordered the ambaffador
to come to him, and faid, ' I confent that you take
along with you as much of your mafter's treafures as
one man can carry; for I will never part with any more.'
The ambaffador made a low bow, and thanked his majefty, and defired him to give orders that they might be
delivered to him. Matapa accordingly fpoke to his trea-
furer, and afterwards went to his palace of retreat, within fome few miles of the city. Fortunio and his attendants went immediately and demanded entrance to the
place where all the treafure was kept. Strongback prefented himfelf, and by his affiftance the ambaffador
carried off moft of the furniture that was in the emperor's
palace; as five hundred gigantic ftatues of gold, coaches
and chariots, and all manner of conveniences; and with
thefe Strong back walked as nimbly as if he had not
above a pound weight on his back.

When the minifters of ftate faw the palace thus gutted,
they made all the hafte imaginable to acquaint the emperor; whofe amazement was not to be expreffed, when
they told him that one man carried all: he cried out he
would not allow it; and immediately ordered his guards
to mount, and to purfue thofe robbers of his treafury.
And though Fortunio was then above ten miles off,

' Fine-ear

Fine ear told him, that he heard a great body of horse coming after them with full speed: and the good Marksman. whose sight was excellent, saw them, just as they themselves came to the river-side. Fortunio said to Trinquit, ' As we have no boats, you must drink up ' this water, that we may pass it.' Which Trinquit readily performed; and Fortunio was for making all possible haste to get away, when his horse bid him not be uneasy, but let the enemy approach. Soon after, they appeared on the banks of the river, and knowing where the fishermen's boats lay, embarked immediately. When the Boisterer began to swell his cheeks, and with a sudden blast over-set the boats, so that not one of that detachment escaped. This happy success puffed them up with so great expectation, that every one began to think of the recompence he deserved, and were for making themselves masters of all the riches they were carrying with them; whereupon a great dispute arose among them: Lightfoot said, ' They had got nothing if he had ' not won the race. ' Well (said Fine-ear) if I had ' not heard you snore, where had you been then?' ' And who would have awaken'd you, if I had not?' (added the Marksman) ' Well (said Strong-back) I can-' not but admire you for your disputes: sure none dare ' pretend to lay so good a claim as myself, since I car-' ried all, and without my assistance, you would not ' have been able to have partaken of them.' ' Say ra-' ther without mine (interrupted Trinquit) since you ' were in a bad plight, if I had not drank your way.' ' Nay, and you were equally in the same danger (said ' the Boisterer) had I not overset the boats,' ' Hither-' to (interrupted Grugeon) I have held my peace, but ' I cannot forbear representing to you, that I opened ' the scene to all these events; for if I had left one crust ' of bread, all had been lost.'

' Friends (said Fortunio, with an air of command) ' you have all done wonders; but we ought to leave it ' to the king to recompense our services; for I should ' be sorry to be rewarded by any other besides him. ' Let us all trust to his generosity, he sent us to fetch

his

' his riches, and not to rob him of them; which thought
' is so shameful, that in my opinion it ought to be
'' smothered: for my own part, I will do so well by you,
'' that you shall have no reason to repine, should it be
' possible for the king to neglect you.'

The seven gifted men penetrated with this remon-
strance of their master, threw themselves at his feet, and
promised that his will should be theirs. After all this,
the lovely Fortunio found himself, as he drew nigh the
city, agitated with a thousand different troubles; the
joy that he had done the king such considerable services,
for whom he had so great an attachment, and the hope
to see him again, and be favourably received by him,
flattered him most agreeably. On the other hand, the
fear of enraging the queen, and being persecuted again
by her and Florida, put him into a heavy concern. In
short, he arrived at the town, where the people, overjoyed
to see so much riches and treasure, followed him to the
palace with great acclamations of joy. The king, who
could scarcely believe such extraordinary news, ran. to
acquaint the queen with it, who was at first struck on a
heap, but recovering herself afterwards, said, ' The
' Gods protect him, therefore I am not surprised he
' should succeed in what he undertakes.' And just as
she made an end of these words, she saw him enter the
room. He informed their majesties of what he had done,
and added, that the treasures were left in the park, no
other place being large enough to hold them: and we
must easily believe the king expressed a great friendship
for so loving and faithful a subject.

The knight's presence, and the advantages of his good
fortune, opened again and dilated those wounds in the
queen's heart which were hardly closed up: she thought
him more charming than ever, and as soon as she was at
liberty to talk with Florida, she renewed her complaints,
' You know (said she) what I have done to ruin him,
' which I thought was the only means to forget him, yet
' his unparalleled good fortune brings him safe home
' again: and whatever reasons I have to despise a man
' so much inferior to me, and who has repaid my senti-
' ments

' timents with the blackest ingratitude, I cannot forbear
' loving him, and am resolved to marry him privately.'
' Marry him, madam! (cried Florida) it is impossible;
' certainly my ears fail me.' ' No (replied the queen)
' you know my intention, and must second me in it.
' I charge you to bring Fortunio this night into my clo-
' set; I will myself declare to him the love I have for
' him.' Florida in despair to be made the instrument
of her mistress's marriage with her lover, forgot nothing
she could say to dissuade the queen from seeing him.
She represented that the king would be angry, should it
be found out, and perhaps might put the knight to
death, or at least would condemn him to perpetual im-
prisonment, where she would never have the sight of
him again: but all her eloquence was in vain: she saw
the queen began to be in a passion, and therefore was
obliged to obey her. She found Fortunio in the gallery
of the palace, ranging in order the golden statues he
brought from the emperor Matapa. She went to him,
with the message from the queen, which made him trem-
ble, and caused Florida no small trouble. ' O heavens!
' (said she) how much I pity you; why could not that
' princess's heart escape you? Alas! I know one not
' half so dangerous, that dares not explain itself.' The
knight would not engage in this new declaration; too
much was he chagrin'd already, but left her, and as he
had no desire to please the queen, dressed himself but indifferently, that she might not think he strove to set himself off; but if he could throw off his jewels and embroi-
deries, he could not do the same by his natural charms.
The queen, for her part, did what she could to heighten
the lustre of her's by an extraordinary fine dress, and
observed with pleasure that Fortunio seemed surprised,
' Appearances (said she) are sometimes so deceitful,
' that I was willing to justify myself concerning what
' you have thought without doubt of my conduct;
' when I engaged the king to send you to the emperor,
' it seemed in all appearance as if I designed to sacrifice
' you; but depend upon it, good knight, I knew what
' would happen, and had no other views than your immortal

' honour.' ' Madam (faid he) you are too much above
' me to need any explanation; I enter not into the
' motives that engaged you; it is enough for me that
' I obey the king my fovereign.' ' You fhew too
' much indifference (added fhe) for the declaration I
' make you of my fentiments; but it is time
' I convince you of my bounty. Come, Fortunio,
' receive my hand as the pledge of my faith.'

The poor knight, quite thunder-ftruck, was twenty
times going to acquaint the queen with his fex, but
durft not ; and anfwering thofe tokens of friendfhip
with great coldnefs, ufed a great many arguments
upon the king's anger, when he fhould know a fubject
durft be fo bold as to contract in his court, fo important a marriage without his confent. After the queen
had endeavoured though in vain, to remove the ob-
ftacles which he feemed to fear, fhe all on a fudden affumed the countenance and voice of a fury,
loaded him with menaces and wrongs, and fought
and fcratched him ; after that, turning her rage upon
herfelf, fhe tore off her hair, claw'd her face and
neck till fhe was all in a gore blood, rent her veil
and head drefs all in pieces, and then called in her
guards, ordered them to carry the wretch, as fhe called
him, to fome dungeon, and in the mean time ran herfelf to the king to demand juftice againft that young
monfter: telling him that he had a long time the
boldnefs to declare his paffion, and that in hopes that
abfence and her feverities might have cured him, fhe had
let no opportunity flip, as he might well obferve, to have
him removed out of the way; but that he was one
that nothing could change: that he himfelf was a witnefs to what extremities his paffion had brought him,
that fhe would have him profecuted with all rigour ;
and that if he refufed her that juftice, fhe fhould
be obliged to ftand upon her own guard for the future.

The manner in which fhe fpoke, amafed the king,
he knew her to be a woman of a moft violent temper, and that withal fhe had a great power, and
could raife great diftractions in the kingdom. For-

C   tunio's

tunio's boldnefs deferved an exemplary punifhment: what was paffed was publicly known to the
whole world, and it was his duty to revenge his fifter's
affront: but alas! on whom was his fury to light?
on a knight who had expofed his life to the greateft dangers, to whom he owed his quiet and all
his treafures, and one, befides, for whom he had a
particular value and love. He would have almoft
loft his own life to fave this dear favourite. He
reprefented to the queen the fervices he had done
both him and the ftate, his youth, and whatever
might induce her to forgive him: but fhe would
give no ear to what he faid, but demanded his life.
The king feeing he could not poffibly avoid his being tried, appointed judges, that he thought to be
the moft mild and fufceptible of tendernefs, who
might put the moft favourable conftruction upon
the letter of the law: but he was miftaken in his
conjectures: the judges were for eftablifhing their
reputation at this poor unhappy knight's expence:
and as it was an affair that would make a great
noife in the world, they armed themfelves with
the utmoft rigour, and condemned Fortunio without hearing him plead for himfelf. His fentence
was to receive three ftabs in the heart, as the heart
was the principal part concerned.

The king dreaded this fentence as much as if it
was to have been pronounced againft himfelf; he
banifhed all the judges, but could not fave his beloved Fortunio, while the queen triumphed in the
punifhment he was to fuffer. The king made ufe
of frefh arguments, which only exafperated her the
more. To be fhort, the day appointed for this
horrid execution came: the knight was brought out
of the prifon where he had been kept from the fpeech
of all perfons, not knowing the crime he was accu-
fed of, but imagined it was fome new perfecution
which his indifference for the queen had brought
upon him; yet what troubled him the moft was,
he thought the king feconded that princefs in what
fhe

she did. In the mean time Florida, inconsolable for the condition to which her lover was reduced, took a resolution of the utmost violence, which was to poison both the queen and herself, if Fortunio was to suffer death so unjustly. As soon as she knew the sentence, despair possessed her soul, and she thought of nothing but the execution of her designs; but it happened that the poison was not prepared so strong as she intended it: Insomuch that though she had given it the queen, she felt not presently the effects of it, but had the lovely knight brought to the great space before the pallace, that she might have the satisfaction of seeing him die. When the executioners had taken him out of the dungeon where he lay, and brought him like a tender lamb going to the slaughter; the first object that his eyes beheld when he came upon the scaffold, was the queen, who thought she could not be too nigh, being desirous to have his blood spurt on her. But alas! the poor king shut himself up in his closet, that he might with more freedom bewail the fate of his dear favourite.

But when they had bound Fortunio, and came to open his breast; how great was the surprise of that numerous assembly, when they saw the white breast of a lovely maid, and knew that she was an innocent damsel unjustly accused! the queen was in so great a confusion, that the poison began to work, and threw her into strong convulsions, out of which she never recovered but to express her bitter regret. In the mean time the people, who loved Fortunio, set her at liberty; and the news was presently carried to the king, who had abandoned himself to malancholy. At that instant joy took place; he ran to the palace, and was charmed to see the new matamorphosis of his dear Fortunio; however, the last sighs and groans of the queen suspended in some measure his transports; but when he came to reflect on her malice, he was not sorry. He resolved to marry this his young heroine, to repay with a crown his great obligations to her; and declared his intentions to her,

which

which we may eafily believe completed the height
of her defires, which where not fo much to be a queen,
as to enjoy the perfon of a prince for whom fhe had
always entertained a moft tender affection.　The day
of celebrating the marriage was fixed; our young
knight laid afide her man's habit, and affumed that
of her own fex, in which fhe appeared a thoufand
times more beautiful.　She confulted her horfe what
adventures fhould happen to her for the future; but
as he could promife none more agreeable, fhe in
gratitude for the great fervices he had done her, built
him a ftable paved with ebony and ivory, and inftead of being litered with ftraw, he lay always on
mats of fattin: and for the feven attendants, they were
all rewarded according to their fervices.

After all this was done, news was brought to our
young queen that comrade was not to be found;
which was no lefs trouble to the king, who adored
her, than to herfelf.　She made inquiry for three days,
all to no purpofe, and on the fourth fhe arofe with
the morning, and went into the garden, which fhe
croffed, and fo into a thick wood, and thence into
a large meadow, called out, 'Comrade! my dear
' Comrade! where art thou? what, do you forfake me!
I have occafion for thy advice,' And as fhe was
talking after this manner, fhe faw all on a fudden
another fun arifing in the weft, which made her ftand
to admire that prodigy; but her amazement ftill
increafed to fee it approach her nigher, and efpe-
cially when fhe knew her horfe again covered with jewels, and prancing before a chariot of pearls and topa-
zes, drawn by four and twenty fheep that were covered with gold fringe inftead of wool: their har-
nefs was crimfon fattin, buckled on with emeralds,
their horns were adorned with carbuncles.　The new
queen knew the fairy her protectrefs in the chariot,
and her father and two fifters, who cried out clap-
ping their hands, and making profeffions of friendfhip, that they were come to her wedding.　Their
fifter, for her part, thought fhe fhould have expired
with

with joy at feeing them again : fhe neither knew what fhe faid or did : but at laft recovering herfelf, fhe got into the chariot, and returned with this pompous equipage to the palace; where every thing was prepared for celebrating the moft magnificent Feaft that ever was made in that kingdom. Thus the enamoured king united himfelf to his fair deliverer, and afforded us this chafming adventure, which has been handed down from one age to another.

THE

STORY

OF

PERFECT LOVE.

IN one of thofe agreeable countries that depend on the empire of the fairies, there reigned the formidable Danamo, who was as knowing in her art, as cruel in her actions, and boafting of the honour of being defended from the celebrated Calipfo, whofe charms had the glory and power of ftarving the famous Ulyfes, and triumping over the prudence of the conquerors of Troy. She was lufty, had a wild look and her pride made her with fome difficulty fubmit to the hard laws of matrimony: for love was not able to reach her heart: but the defign of uniting a flourishing kingdom to that she was queen of, and another she had ufurped, made her confent to marry an old neighbouring king, who died fome few years after their marriage, and left the fairy a daughter called Azira, who was very ugly: but appeared not fo in the eye of Danamo, who thought her charming, perhaps becaufe like herfelf. She was to be the queen of three kingdoms, which circumftance qualified all her defects, and caufed her to be afked in the marriage by the moft powerful princes of the neighbouring countries.

This together with the blind fondnefs of Danamo, rendered her vanity infupportable, fince fhe was defired with an ardour which fhe did in no wife deferve. But as Danamo thought of nothing but rendering the princefs's happinefs compleat, fhe brought up in her palace a young prince, her Brother's fon who was called Parcinus: he had a noble air, a delicate fhape, a fine head of hair, fo admirably white, that love himfelf might have been jealous of his power: for that god never had golden fhafts more fure of triumphing over hearts without refiftance, than the eyes of Parcinus. He did every thing well, danced and fung extraordinary fine, and gained all the prizes at tournaments, whenever he contended for them.

This young prince was the delight of the court; and Danamo, who had her defigns, was not againft the refpect and value they fhewed him. The king, his father, was the fairy's brother, whom fhe declared war againft without any pretence whatfoever.

This king fought courageoufly at the head of his troops; but what could an army do againft fo powerful a fairy as Lanamo? who fuffered the victory not to balance long after her brother's death, who was killed in the action, with one ftroke of her wand difperfed her enemies and became miftrefs of the kingdom.

Parcinus was then an infant in arms: they brought
him

him to Danamo; for it would have been in vain
to have concealed him from a fairy: he had then such
engaging smiles, that they won all hearts: and Danamo caressing him, in a few days after carried him
home with her to her own kingdom.

The prince was about eighteen years old, when
the fairy willing to execute what she had so long
designed, resolved to marry him with her daughter;
and not doubting but the prince, who was born one,
but by his misfortunes made a subject, would be o-
verjoyed to become one day a sovereign of three em-
pires, sent for the princess, and discovered to her
the choice she had made.

The princess harkened to this discourse with an
emotion that made the fairy think that this resolution in favor of Parcinus, displeased her daughter.—
I see (said she to her, observing her disorder increase)
‘ that your ambition carries you so far, that you
‘ would add to your empire the dominions of one
‘ of these kings, who have demanded you so often,
‘ But what kings may not Parcinus overcome? his
‘ courage is beyond every thing: the subjects of a
‘ prince so accomplished, may some time revolt in his
‘ favor; and by giving you to him, I make sure of
‘ the possession of his kingdom. And for his person,
‘ we need not speak of that; you know the proudest
‘ beauties are not able to resist his charms.

The princess casting herself suddenly at the feet
of the fairy, interrupted her discourse, and confessed
to her, that her heart had not had the power to with-
stand that young victor, so famous for his conquests
‘ But (added she blushing) I have given the insen-
‘ sible Parcinus a thousand marks of my tender-
‘ ness, which he received with a coldness that makes
‘ me despair.’ It was because he durst not raise his
‘ thoughts up to you (replied the proud fairy) he
‘ was without doubt afraid of displeasing me; I know
‘ his respect.’

This flattering opinion was too agreeable to the princess's inclination and vanity, for her not to be per-

perfuaded to it. In fhort, the fairy fent for Parcinus, who came to her in a magnificent chariot, where
fhe and the princefs her daughter, waited for him :
when fhe faid to him, as foon as fhe faw him, ' Call
' all your courage to your aid : I fent for you not
' to continue your misfortune, but for your good:
' reign, Parcinus: and to compleat your hapinefs,
' reign by marrying my daughter.' I, madam ! (cried
' the young prince in an amafement, wherein it was
' eafy to perceive his joy had not the greateft fhare)
' I marry the princefs, (continued he, falling back
' fome fteps) alas ! what god concerns himfelf in my
' fate, not to leave it to him alone from whom I
' afk affiftance.

These words were pronounced by the prince with
an heat which his heart had too great a fhare in to
be withftood by his reafon. The fairy thought that
this unlooked for happinefs had put him befide himfelf ; but the princes loved, and love makes lovers
more penetrating than wifdom itfelf. 'What god, Par-
' cinus' (faid fhe to him with diforder) do you fo
' tenderly implore the affiftance of ; I know too well
' I have no fhare in the vows you offer up to him.'

The young prince, had had time to recover his
firft furprife, and who knew he had been guilty of
an imprudence in what he had faid, fummoned all
his wit to the aid of his heart, and anfwered the
princefs more gallantly than fhe hoped for ; and thanked
the fairy with an air of grandeur, that fhewed him
not only worthy the empire offered him, but that of
the whole world.

Danamo, and her proud daughter, who were both
fatisfied with this difcourfe, fettled all things before
they went out of the clofet: the fairy deferred the
day of the nuptials, only to give the court time to
prepare themfelves on fo great an occafion. After
this, the news of Parcinus's marriage with Azira,
was fpread all about the court; and the courtiers came
in crowds to congratulate the prince.

Parcinus received all their compliments with an
air

air of coldnefs, which very much furprifed his new
fubjeĉts, that he fhould appear chagrined and out
of humour: all the reft of the day he was perplexed
with the congratulations of the whole court, and the
continual declarations of Azira's paffion.

¡ What a condition was the young prince in, who was feized
with a lively grief? the day feem'd to him a thoufand
times longer than ordinary. The impatient Parcinus longed for night, which at laft came; when with
hafte he left that place where he had fuffered fo much,
and went to his own apartment; and after having
fent all his attendants away, opened a door that went
into the gardens of the palace, which he croffed, followed only by a young flave.

A fine but fmall river ran at the end of thefe
gardens, and feparated the fairy's palace from a caftle
flanked with four towers, and furrounded by a deep
ditch that was filled by the river: thither flew parcinus's wifhes and defires.

A wonder was fhut up in it, which treafure, Danamo had carefully guarded. It was a young princefs, her fifter's daughter, who when fhe died left
her to the care of the fairy; her beauty worthy of
the admiration of the whole world, appearing too dangerous for Danamo to permit her to be feen nigh
Azira. Sometimes the charming Irolita, which was
her name, was fuffered to come to the palace to fee
the fairy, and the princefs her daughter; but was never
allowed to appear in public: yet her charms though
concealed, were not unknown to the world.

The prince Parcinus faw her with the princefs
Azira, and adored her from that very moment.—
Their nearnefs of blood gave this young prince no
privilege with Irolita: for after fhe was grown up,
the mercilefs Danamo permitted none to fee her.

In the mean time, Parcinus burnt with a raging
flame, which the charms of Irolita had kindled: fhe
was about fourteen years old, her beauty was per-
feĉt, her hair of a fine brown, her complexion bloom-
ing as the fpring; her mouth delicate, her teeth admi-

rably white and even; and her smiles engaging,
her eyes were of a fine hazzle colour, and piercing,
and her looks seemed to speak a thousand things her
young heart as yet knew nothing of.

She had been brought up in great solitude, nigh the
fairy's palace, in the castle where she lived: but saw
no more of the world than if she had been in a desert. Danamo's orders where so exactly obeyed, that
the fair Irolita passed her days only among those women appointed her, whose number was very small,
but yet as many as were necessary in so lonely and
retired a court; however, Fame, which regarded not
Danamo, published so many wonders of this young
princess, that persons at the greatest distance from
the court, offered themselves to be with the young
Irolita. And her presence belied not what fame had
reported, since they always found her worthy their
admiration.

A governante of great wit and knowledge, former-
ly attached to the princess her mother, lived with
her, and often groaned under the rigours of Danamo toward the charming Irolita: she was called Mana;
and her desire of setting the princes at liberty and
restoring her to her right and dignity, made her yield
to Parcinus's love. It was then three years since he
was introduced into the castle in the habit of a slave;
at which time he found her in the garden, and discovered to her his passion; and as she was then but
a child, she loved Parcinus only as a brother. Mana, who was never absent long from her, surprised
the young prince in the garden one day, when he
acquainted her with his love for the princess, and
the design he had formed to lose his life or restore
her liberty? and seeking, by shewing himself to his
subjects, a glorious revenge on Danamo, and placed
Irolita on the throne. As the rising merit of Parcinus was capable of rendering the most difficult pro-
jects credible, and was the only means to deliver
Irolita, Mana suffered him to come somtimes to the
castle, when it was night; but never let him see the
princess,

princefs, except in her prefence. He, with his tender difcourfe, and his conftant fedulities, endeavoured to infpire in her as violent a paffion as his own.
Thus employed for three years, he went almoft every
night to the caftle, and fpent all the days in nothing
but thinking of the princefs. But to return to where
we left him croffing the gardens, followed by a flave,
and pierced with grief at the refolutions of the fairy;
when he came to the river-fide, a gilded boat which Azira
fometimes to k the air in, that was faftened to the bank ferved to carry this amorous prince over. The flave rowed, and as foon as Parcinus had got up a filken ladder,
that was thrown out from off a little terrafs, that fronted
the caftle, the faithful flave rowed the boat back again,
where he waited for the fignal he made him, which was
to fhew him a lighted flambeaux from off the terrafs.—
That night the prince took his ufual tour; the filken ladder was let down, and he entered without any obfticle the
young Irolita's chamber, whom he found laid on the bed
all in tears: but the beauty that appeared in that melancholy pofture, had an extraordinary effect on the prince!
    ‘ What ails my princefs? (faid he, falling on his
‘ knees by the bedfide whereupon fhe lay? what could
‘ caufe thefe precious tears? alas! (continued he figh-
‘ ing) have I yet new misfortunes to hear?’ the tears
and fighs of thefe young lovers were intermixed, and
they were forced to vent their paffion before they could
tell the caufe of their grief. At length the young prince
defired Irolita to tell him what new feverity the fairy
had ufed to her, ‘ She will marry Azira (anfwered the
‘ beautiful Irolita blufhing) which, of all her cruelties,
is the moft painful to me.’ ‘ O my dear princefs (cried
‘ the prince) you fear left I fhould marry Azira: my
‘ fate is a thoufand times more kind than I thought it.’
‘ Can you praife fate, (replied the young Irolita, lan-
‘ guifhingly) when it is ready to feparate us? I cannot
‘ exprefs the torments, the dread of that makes me feel.
‘ O! Parcinus, you are in the right, the love of a lover,
‘ and that of a brother is quite different. The amorous
prince thought to thank his fortune; he never till then

knew

knew the love the young Irolita had for him : and, in
short, could no longer doubt of the good fortune of having infpired fuch tender fentiments into the princefs.
This happinefs, which he did not expect, roufed up all
his hopes. 'No (cried he in a tranfport) I defpare not
' now of overcoming our misfortunes, fince I am affu-
' red of your tendernefs. Let us fly, my princefs, let
' us avoid the rage of Danamo, and her hateful Daugh-
' ter ; let us not truft to fo fatal an abode ; love alone
' will make us happy.' 'Should I go away with you
' (replied the princefs with furprife) what would the
' world fay of my flight ?' Lay afide thefe vain reflec-
' tions, (fair Irolita) interrupted the impatient Parci-
' nus ; every circumftance urges us to leave this place ;
' let us go——' 'But where will you go! (replied the
prudent Mana, who was always with them, and who,
lefs engaged than thofe young lovers, forefaw all the
difficulties in their flight) 'I will give you an account of
' my defign (replied the prince) but how did you hear
' fo foon the news from the fairy's court ? A relation
' of mine (anfwered Mana) writ to me as foon as it was
' wifpered about the palace, and I thought it my duty
' to inform the princefs of it.' 'And what have I endu-
' red fince ? (replied the lovely Irolita) no, Parcinus,
' I cannot live without you.' The young prince tranfported with love, and charmed with thefe words, kiffed
Irolita's hand with an ardour and tendernefs, that had
all the thanks of a firft and moft agreeable favour. Day
began to appear, and informed Parcinus too foon that
it was time he retired, when he affured the princefs he
would come again the next night, and impart to her his
project : he got to the boat and flave again, and retired
to his apartment. He was fo overjoyed with the pleafure of being beloved by the fair Irolita, and agitated by
the difficulties he forefaw they fhould meet with in their
flight, that fleep could not calm that uneafinefs, nor
make him forget a moment of his happinefs.

　It was hardly morning, when a dwarf entered his
chamber, and prefented him with a fine fcarf from the
princefs Azira, who by a billet more tender than he
wifhed

wifhed for, defired him to wear from that day that fcarf.
He fent an anfwer, which very much confounded him ;
but he was obliged to it, to deliver Irolita, and to con-
ftrain himfelf for her liberty. When he had fent Azira's
Dwarf away, a giant came from Danamo, and prefented him with a fabre of extraordinary beauty, the han-
dle of which was of one fingle ftone, more beautiful
than a diamond, and which gave a great light in the
night ; on this fabre were engraved thefe words.

For the hand of a conqueror.

Parcinus was mightily pleafed with the fairy's prefent,
and went and thanked her with that and the fcarf on.
The tendernefs of Irolita fufpended all difquiets ; fhe
had raifed in his heart that fweet and perfect fatisfaction
fuccefsful love feels : a pleafant air appeared in all his
actions, which Azira attributed to her charms, and the
fairy to Parcinus's ambition : the day was fpent in pleafures and diverfions, which in no wife diminifhed the
infupportable length Parcinus thought it.

In the evening they took the air in the gardens of the
palace, and on the fame river fo well known to the
prince, who in going in the boat, felt a fenfible concern,
to fee what difference there was between the pleafures
it ufed to give him, and the cruel torments he then endured. Parcinus could not forbear looking often at the
habitation of the charming Irolita, who never appeared
when the fairy or Azira were on the water. That Princefs, who watched all the actions of the prince, obferved
that his eyes were often turned towards the caftle.—
‘ What do you look at, prince? (faid fhe) in the midft
‘ of honours done you, is Irolita's prifon worthy your
‘ regard?' ‘Yes, madam (replied the prince very impru-
‘ dently) I am fenfible of the fufferings of thofe who de-
‘ ferve them not.' You are too compaffionate (anfwer-
‘ ed Azira difdainfully) but to eafe you of your pain,
‘ I can tell you, Irolita will not be long a prifoner.'—
‘ And what will become of her (replied the young prince
fhort) ‘ The queen will marry her in five days to the
prince

'prince Brutus (returned Azira:) he is of our blood you
'know, and according to the intentions of the queen,
'he will the next day after their marriage carry Irolita
'into a fortress, from whence she will never return to
'court.' 'What! (said the prince, in an extraordinary
'disorder) will the queen give that beautiful princess
'to so hideous a prince, whose ill qualities exceed his
'deformity? what cruelty is this?' (This last word
came from him against his will, but he could no longer
conceal his resentment. 'I thought that you, of all
'people, Parcinus (answered the princess haughtily)
'should not complain of Danamo's cruelties.' This
conversation, without doubt, had been pushed too far for
the young prince, whose business it was to dissemble, if
the attendants of Azira had not come up, and the fairy,
appeared on the river side. Azira returned to the fairy,
and Parcinus coming out of the boat, feigned to be sick,
that he might have the more liberty to go and complain,
without any witness of his new misfortunes.

The fairy, and above all Azira, shewed a great unea-
siness for his being ill. He retired, accusing fate a thousand times for the misfortunes that threatened the charming Irolita, abandoning himself to all his grief and tenderness; but beginning at length to recover those disorders
faithful lovers are so subject to, he writ in the most moving expressions his love could dictate, to one of his aunts,
whose name was Favourable; who was a fairy as well
as Danamo, but one who took as much pleasure in com-
forting and assisting the unfortunate, as Danamo did
in making them so. He told her to what a cruel condition his love and fortune had reduced him; and not
daring to leave Danamo's court without discovering his
designs, he sent his faithful slave with it.

When every body was retired, he left his apartment
as usual, and crossing the gardens alone, went into the
boat, without knowing whether he could row or not; but
what will not love teach us? he rowed as well as the most
expert seaman, and got into the castle, where he was
very much surprised to find Mana only, and she all in
tears, in the princess's chamber, 'What is the matter
                                                      with

' with you, Mana (faid the prince in hafte) and where
' is my dear Irolita ?' ' Alas! fir, (faid Mana) fhe is not
' here, a troop of the queen's guards, and fome woman,
' carried her away from this caftle three or four hours
' ago.' Parcinus heard not the end of thefe words, but
fwooned away as foon as he underftood the princefs was
gone. Mana took a great deal of pains to bring him
to himfelf again, which was no fooner done, but falling
fuddenly into a paffion, he drew a little dagger he wore
in his girdle, and had pierced his heart, had not the wife
Mana, holding his arm, and falling on her knees, faid
' What, fir, will you forfake Irolita ; live to deliver her
' from Danamo's rage. Alas! without you, where will
' fhe find fuccour againft the cruelty of the fairy ?' thefe
words fufpended the unhappy prince's defpair : ' Alas!
' (replied he fhedding tears, which all his courage could
' not reftrain) where is my princefs? yes, Mana, I will
' live to have the fad fatisfaction of dying for her, and
' expiring in revenging her of her enemies.' After thefe
words, Mana begged of him to leave that difmal place,
to avoid frefh misfortunes. 'Go prince (faid fhe) how
' know we but the fairy has fombody here to give her
' an account of what paTes ? take care of a life fo dear
' to a princefs you adore.' After this advice, the
prince went away, and returned to his own apartment
with all the grief fo unhappy and tender a paffion could
infpire. He paffed the night on a couch he threw himfelf on when he went in, where day furprifed him ;
which had appeared fome hours, when he heard a noife
at his chamber door. He ran with that eager impatience we generally exprefs, when we expect news, wherein our hearts are fo much concerned ; and found that
his people had brought him a man who wanted to fpeak
with him in hafte, and whom he knew to be one of Mana's
relations, he gave Parcinus a letter, who went into his
clofet to hide the trouble it might give him; where he
opened it, and found thefe words

Mana,

MANA,

To the greatest Prince in the world.

'BE assured, sir, our princess is in safety; if that
' expression may be allowed, while in the power of
' her enemy; she has asked Danamo for me, who has
' suffered me to be with her; there is a guard in the
' palace. Yesterday the queen sent for her into her clo-
' set, and ordered her proudly to look on the prince
' Brutus, as one that was to be her husband in a few
' days, and presented to her that prince, so unworthy
' of being your rival. The princess was so much afflict-
' ed, that she made her no answer, but by tears, which
' are not yet dried up. You, sir, must find out means,
' if possible, to assist her against such pressing Misfor-
' tunes.'

At the bottom of the letter these words were written.
blotted, and with a trembling hand.

'HOW much I pity you my dear prince! your
' calamities are more grievous to me than my own:
' I spare your tenderness the recital of what I have en-
' dured since yesterday; why should I trouble the re-
' pose of your life? alas! without me you might have
' been happy.'

What joy and grief did the prince feel? what kisses
he gave this invaluable token of the divine Irolita's
love? he was so much beside himself, that he had much
ado to return a suitable answer; he thanked the prudent
Mana, informed the princess of the assistance he expected from the fairy Favourable, and said a thousand
things on his grief and love: afterwards he gave the
letter to Mana's relation and with it a present of fine
jewels of an inestimable value, to recompense him for
the pleasure he had done him. He was scarcely gone,
when the queen and the princess Azira sent to know how
the prince did. It was easy to know, by his looks,
that he was not well; they pressed him to go to bed,
which

which he agreed to, thinking he fhould be lefs conftrain-
ed then if he went to the fairy.

After dinner the queen went herfelf to fee him, and
fpoke to him of Irolita's marriage with the prince Brutus, as a thing refolved on. Parcinus, who had at laft
refolved to reftrain himfelf to carry on his defigns the
better, feeming to approve of the fairy's intentions, and
defired her only to ftay till he had recovered, becaufe
he had a great mind to be at the folemnity. The fairy
and Azira, who defpaired at his ficknefs, and promifed him
what he afked; by which means he retarded the difmal
nuptials of Irolita for fome days. the converfation he
had on the water with Azira forwarded the misfortune
of the princefs he loved fo tenderly; for Azira had given
the queen an account of his difcourfe and his compaffion
for Irolita. And the queen, who never delayed the
execution of her will, fent that evening for Irolita, and
refolved with Azira, to finifh the marriage of that princefs, and to haften her departure before Parcinus had
a more eftablifhed authority? but in the mean time,
before the expiration of the time, the faithful flave arrived. How great was Parcinus's joy, to find in the letter
Favourable had wrote, marks of her compaffion and
friendfhip for him and Irolita! fhe fent him a little ring,
compofed of four different metals, gold, filver, brafs,
and iron: this ring had the power of fecuring them four
times againft the perfecutions of the cruel Danamo:
and Favourable affured the prince, that the wicked fairy
could not purfue them oftener than the ring had power
to fave them. This good news reftored the young
prince to his health; he fent in all hafte for Mana's relation and gave him a letter, that informed Irolita of the
happy fuccefs they might flatter themfelves withal.—
They had no time to lofe, the queen was for comfum-
mating prince Brutus's marriage in three days, and that
fame night Azira made a ball, and Irolita was to be
there. Parcinus could not think of being negligent on
that occafion: he dreffed himfelf in a magnificent fuit,
and appeared a thoufand times mo e bright than the
day; but durft not fpeak to Irolita, except with his eyes,
which

which often met thofe of that fair princefs. Irolita had
on the noblef dref imaginable : the fairy had given her
very fine jewels ; and as fhe had but four days to ftay in
her palace, refolved to treat her as fhe ought to be.—
Her beauty not ufed to be fet off with fuch ornaments,
feemed wonderful to all, and much more to the amorous
Parcinus, who thought, by the joy that he faw in her
bright eyes, fhe had received his letter.' The prince
Brutus talked often with Irolita ; but he appeared of fo
ill a mien unto the gold and jewels he was, loaded with,
that he was not a rival worthy the young prince's jealoufy.
The ball was almoft over, when Parcinus, tranfported
with his love, defired with great ardour, the liberty of
talking a moment with the princefs. ' Cruel queen,
' and thou hateful Azira, (faid he to himfelf) will you de-
' prive me yet longer of the charming pleafure of tel-
' ling the fair Irolita a thoufand times how I adore her ?
' why leave you not, you jealous witneffes of my happi-
' nefs, the place, fince love can only triumph in your
' abfence ;' he had hardly formed this wifh, but the
fairy finding herfelf a little out of order, called Azira,
and went with her into the next room, whither prince
Brutus followed them : Parcinus had then the ring on
his finger the fairy Favourable had fent him. He ought
to have preferved the fuccours given him for more pref-
fing occafions, but violent love and prudence are feldom companions ; the young prince thought, by the fairy's
and Azira's departure, that the ring began to favour
his love : he flew to the charming Irolita, and fpoke to
her of his paffion in the moft touching and eloquent
expreffions ; when he perceived that he had made ufe of
Favourable's charms fillily, but could not repent of an
imprudence which gained him the pleafure of entertaining his dear Irolita : they refolved on their place and
hour to put an end to their cruel flavery the next day.
The fairy and Azira returned again fome time after,
Parcinus parted with no fmall regret from Irolita, and
looking on his ring, perceived that the iron was
mixed with the other metals, and faw very well that
he had but three wifhes to make, which he refolved to
employ

employ better than the first for his princefs? but trusted
none with his departure, but his faithful flave. The
next day he appeared to the queen very eafy, and
more pleafant than ordinary: he paffed fome compliments on the prince Brutus upon his marriage, and did
it in a manner capable of removing all fufpicions they
might entertain of his paffion. At two o' clock in the
morning he went to the fairy's park, where he found his
faithful flave, who, according to his matter's orders had
brought four of his horfes. The prince waited a little,
when the lovely Irolita came wearied, and leaning on
Mana ; for that young princefs endured fo much in the
walk, that love alone, without Danamo's cruelties, and
the ill qualities of prince Brutus, would not have been
capable to have made her undertake it. It was then
fummer, the night was clear, and the moon and ftars
fhined fo bright, that it was as light as day. The prince
made up in hafte towards. her, kiffed her hand, for it
was not a place to talk in, and helped her on her horfe,
for fhe rid wonderfully well, it being one of her amufe-
ments to take horfe with her maids and ride into a little
wood, fome diftance from the caftle, which the fairy
fuffered her to take the air in. Afterwards Parcinus
mounted his horfe, and Mana and the flave theirs.
The young prince drawing the brillaint fabre the fairy
gave him, fwore to the fair Irolita, to adore her all his
life, and to die, if neceffary, in her defence. After thefe
words they went away, and the zephirs feemed to corref-
pond with them, or to take Irolita for Flora, by always
attending them.

In the mean time, day difcovered to Danamo a piece
of news fhe little expected. The ladies who where about
Irolita, where amazed that fhe flept fo long; but obey-
ing the prudent Mana, who lay in the fame chamber
with Irolita, from whence they went out at a little back-
door, that led them into a court of the palace, very little
frequented, by a door that was in Irolita's clofet, and
was nailed up : but in two or three nights they found out
the means to open it. In fhort, the queen fent for Irolita :
in obedience to the fairy, they knocked at the princefs's
chamber

chamber door, and nobody anfwered. But when the prince Brutus arrived, who came to conduct the princefs to the queen, he was very much furprifed: He broke open the door, and went in, and feeing the little door in the clofet forced, he no longer doubted of the princefs's flight. When the news was carried to the queen, fhe fhaked with anger, and ordered them to fearch every where for Irolita; but it was all in vain, nobody could give any account of her. The prince Brutus himfelf went to feek after her, and fent the fairy's guards with all fpeed on the roads he thought they might take. In the mean time, Azira obferved that Parcinus did not appear in this general confternation: and jealoufy open- ing her eyes, fhe fent in hafte to him, and began to think that the prince had taken Irolita away. The fairy herfelf could not believe it: but on confulting her books, fhe found Azira's fufpicion to be a matter of fact. In the mean time, the princefs having learned that Parcinus was not in his apartment, nor the palace, fent to the caftle where Irolita had been fo long, to fee if fhe could find any thing wereby fhe might juftify or condemn the prince. The prudent Mana had taken care to leave nothing that might difcover Irolita's correfpondence with Parcinus, but Azira's fcarf, which was f und on the couch he fwooned on, and had been untied while he was in that condition; and which neither the prince nor Mana, who where full of grief, perceived. What did not the haughty Azira feel at the fight of that fcarf? her love and pride fuffered both alike; fhe afflicted her- felf to excefs, and fent all the fervants of Irolita and the prince to prifon. The ingratitude the queen thought Parcinus had fhewed her, pufhed her natural rage to the laft extremity. She would willingly have given one of her kingdoms to have been revenged on thofe two lovers, who at the fame time where purfued on all fides: prince Brutus and his troop met with frefh horfes every where by the fairy's order, whereas thofe of Parci- nus's where tired, and anfwered not the impatience of their Mafter. At the further fide of a Foreft he over- took them: the firft motion of the prince was to go and fight

fight that unworthy rival ; he was riding up to him with
his fabre drawn, when Irolita cried out, ' prince feek
' not an unprofitable danger, obey the orders of the fairy
' Favourable.' Thefe words gave a check to Parcinus's
rage, who to obey the princefs and the fairy, wifhed the
princefs was in fafety againft the perfecutions of the
cruel queen. He had fcarcely made his wifh, but the
earth opened between him and his rival; a little ugly
man, magnificently dreffed, appeared, and made a fign
to him to follow him. The defent was eafy on their
fide, he went down on horfeback, with Irolita and
Manz, and the flave, and the earth clofed. Brutus,
furprifed at fo extraordinary an event, went in hafte to
give Danamo an account of it ; and in the mean time
our young lovers followed the little man through a dark
road, that led to a large palace, lighted with flambeaux
and lamps. They alighted from off their horfes, went
into a prodigious large hall, fupported by fhining pillars of earth, covered with ornaments of gold ; a little
man loaded with jewels, fat on a throne of gold at the
bottom of the hall, with a great number of people like
himfelf about him, who conducted the prince to that place
who, as foon as he appeared with the charming Irolita,
the little man arofe from his throne, and faid to him,
' Come, prince, the great fairy Favourable, who has
' been a long time one of my friends, hath defired me
' to fecure you againft the cruelties of Danamo. I am
' king of the Gnomes, you and the princefs are welcome
' to my palace.' Parcinus thanked him for his affiftance. The king and all his fubjects where enchanted
at the beauty of Irolita ; they took her for a ftar that
came to brighten their abode, and ferved up a magnificent entertainment. The king of the Gnomes paid
them all manner of refpect, in harmonious concert, but
fomewhat wild was the diverfion of the night, where
they fung the charms of Irolita, and repeated feveral
times thefe verfes ;

What ftar is this that thus our fight invades,
And darts fuch beams on thefe our gloomy fhades ?
Which, whlie its luftre fondly we admire,
Dazzles our eyes, and fets our hearts on fire.

After the mufick was done, they led the prince and princefs, each into a magnificent room, and Mana and the faithful flave followed them. The next day they fhewed them the king's palace, who difpofed of all the riches of the earth; nothing could be added to that treafure, which was a confufed mafs of fine things unformed. The prince and princefs remained eight days in this fubterraneous abode; Favourable had ordered the king of the Gnomes, during that time, to make the princefs and her lover gallant and magnificent entertainments. The night before their departure, the king, to immortalize the memory of their refidence in his empire, had their two ftatues erected in gold on each fide his throne, on pedeftals of white marble, with thefe words writ in letters of diamonds on the pedeftal of the princefs's ftatue:

We defire no more the fight of the fun;
  We have feen this prince,
Who is brighter and more beautiful.

And on the pedeftal of the princefs's ftatue

  To the immortal honour
Of the goddefs of beauty,
  Who defcended here,
Under the name of Irolita.

The ninth day the prince had very fine horfes given him, whofe trappings where of gold, laid over with diamonds, and left, with his fmall troop, the dark abode of the Gnomes, after paying their acknowledgments to their king, and found himfelf in the fame place where prince Brutus attacked him? and looking on his ring, perceived only the Silver and brafs. He purfued his way with the charming, Irolita, and haftened to arrive at the habitation of the fairy Favourable, where they were to be in fafety: when all on a fudden coming out of a vale, they met a troop of Danamo's guards, who where ftill in fearch after them; and were juft ready to fall on them; when the prince wifhed, and prefently
                                        there

there appeared a great fpace of water between them and
the fairy troops. A beautiful nymph half naked, rofe
up in the middle of the water, in a boat of ruſhes, laced
together, and making towards the ſhore, defired the
prince and his beautiful miſtreſs to come into it; who,
with Mana and the ſlave, left their horſes in the field,
and went into the boat, which funk under water, and
made the guards think they chofe rather to drown themfelves, than fall into their hands. Immediately they
found themfelves in a palace, the walls of which where
great drops of water, which falling continually, made
halls, chambers, clofets, and encompaffed gardens, where
a thouſand fpoutings of water, of odd Figuies, formed
the defign of parterres. None but Naids could live in
this palace, fo fine and fingular as it was; therefore to
afford the prince and the fair Irolita a more folid habitation, the Naid that conducted them, carried them
into grottos of ſhell-work, compofed of coral, pearls, and
all the riches of the fea. Their beds were of mofs,
a hundred dolphins guarded Irolita's grot, and twenty
whales the prince's. The Naids admired at their return, the beauty of Irolita? and moreover, a Triton
grew jealous of the prince's looks and care: they gave
them in the prince's grotto, a collation of fine fruits;
twelve Syrons came to charm, by their ſweet voices, the
trouble of the prince and Irolita, and fung the follow-
ing fong;

Wherever love our hearts conveys,
He makes us happy different ways :
Perfect lovers, triumph in your chains,
And let your paſſions ſtill furmount your pains.

At night there was an entertainment, confiſting wholly
of fiſh, of an extraordinary fize and exquifite taſte.——
After this repaſt, the Naids danced in habits of fiſh ſcales
of different colours, which was very fine; bodies of Tri-
tons, with inſtruments unknown to men, compofed a
fymphony, which was odd, but new and very agreeable.
Parcinus and the fair Irolita were four days in this em-

empire; the fifth day the Naids came in crowds to con duct the prince and princefs ; which two lovers went into a Boat of one entire fhell, and the Naids halfout of the water, accompanied them to the river-fide, where Parcinus found his horfes again, and fet forward with fpeed ; when looking on his ring, he perceived only the brafs ; but they were then nigh Favourable's palace. They travelled three days, when on the fourth, at fun-rifing, they perceived men in arms, who, when they came near, appeared to be the prince Brutus and his troop, whom Danamo had fent again to purfue them, with orders not to leave them, if they found them, nor to ftir off the fpot, where any thing extraordinary fhould fall out ; and above all, to endeavour to engage the prince to fight. Danamo knew very well, after what Brutus had told her, that a fairy protected the prince and princefs ; but her knowledge was fo great, that fhe defpaired not of overcoming them by more pewerful charms. Prince Brutus overjoyed to fee the prince and Irolita again, whom he fought after with fo much diligence, rid with his fword in his hand up to Parcinus, to endeavour to fight him, according to Danamo's orders. The young prince drew his fword with fo fierce an air, that Brutus repented more than once of his undertaking ; but Parcinus perceiving Irolita all in tears, moved with compaffion at that fight made his fourth wifh, and prefently their arofe a great fire up to the fkies, which feparated Parcinus from his enemy. This fire made prince Brutus and his troop fall back. The young prince and Irolita, who were always attended by the faithful flave and Mana, found themfelves in a palace, the fight of which, being all fire, at firft frightened Irolita ; but fhe was foon encouraged, when fhe perceived fhe felt no greater heat than that of the fun, and that this fire had only the flaming quality, and not thofe others, which render it infupportable. A great many young and handfome perfons, richly cloathed. came from whence the flames feemed to rife, to receive the princefs and her lover. One of them, whom they judged to be the queen of that place, by the refpects paid to her, faid, ' Come, char-

ming

' charming princefs, and you lovely Parcinus you are
' in the kingdom of Salamanders: I am the queen, and
' with pleafure am charged by Favourable to conceal
' you feven days in my palace: I wifh only your abode
' here was to be long.r.'   After thefe words. fhe carried
them into a large apaitment all on fire, like the reft
of the palace, and which gave as great a light as the fun.
That night they fupped with the queen, and had a noble entertainment: after it was over, they went on a
terras, to fee an artificial fire of wonderful beauty,
and a very fingular defign, which was prepared in a
great court before the Salamander's palace.   Twelve
loves were on pillars of marble, of different colours: fix
of them feemed ready to draw their bows, and the fix
others held out a great plate, whereon thefe words were
written in charecters of fire:

Where'er fair Irolite *appears,*
A glorious conqueft there fhe bears:
Our raging flames and hotteft fire,
Fall fhort of what her eyes infpire
So great's the torment of defire.

The young Irolita blufhed at her own glory, and
Parcinus was overjoyed that fhe was thought as handfome
as fhe appeared to him.   In the mean time the cupids
drew their arrows of fire, which croffing in the air, formed
in a thoufand places the cypher and name of Irolita,
and carried it up to the heavens.   The feven days they
ftayed in this palace where fpent in pleafures and diverfions.   Parcinus obferved, that all the Salamanders had
a great deal of fpirit, and a charming vivacity, were all
gallant and amorous, and that the queen herfelf was not
exempt from that paffion, fince fhe was in love with a
young Salamander of extraordinary beauty.   The
eighth day they left with regret an abode fo agreeable to
their tendernefs, and found themfelves in a fine field
where Parcinus looking on his ring, found on the four
metals mixed together, thefe words engraved:

You wifhed too foon.
                  D   Thefe

These words afflicted the prince and young princess, but they were so nigh Favourable's habitation, that they hoped to reach it that day. This thought suspended their grief, they went forwards, calling on fortune and love, too often deceitful guides. The prince Brutus followed the fairy's orders, never stirred from the place where the fire separated them, but lay encamped behind a wood, when his centinals, who kept continual watch, informed him that the prince and princess appeared on the plain again. He mounted his troop, and came up by night with the unfortunate prince and divine Irolita. Parcinus was not in the least dismayed at the great number of those who attacked him all at once: he flew on them with a courage that terrified them : ' I fulfil my ' promise, fair Irolita (said he, drawing his sabre) I will ' dye for you, or deliver you from your enemies.' After these words, he struck the first he met, and felled him at his feet : but, O grief unexpected! that sabre which he had of the fairy, broke into a thousand pieces. It was what the fairy expected from the combat with the young prince ; for when she gave any arms, she charmed them in such a manner, that when they were made use of against herself, they should break at the first blow into a thousand pieces. Parcinus thus disarmed, could not long resist the numbers that surrounded him : took him, loaded him with chains, and made the young Irolita undergo the same fate. O ! Fairy Fa- ' vourable (cried the prince melancholy) abandon me ' to all the rage of Danamo, but save the fair Irolita.' ' You have disobeyed the fairy (answered a young man ' of surprising beauty, who appeared in the air) you ' must endure the punishment ; if you had not been ' so prodigal of Favourable's assistance, we had preserved ' you against the cruelties of Danamo. The whole king- ' dom of the Sylphs are vexed that they had not the ' glory of rendering so charming a prince, and so beau- ' tiful a princess, happy.' After this he disappeared. Parcinus groaned at his imprudence , he appeared insensible of his own misfortunes, but was cruelly agitated with those of Irolita : and the regret of having contribu-
ted

ted to them, had made him to die away for grief, if
fate had not prepared more cruel torments for him to
undergo. The young Irolita shewed a courage worthy
her illustrious blood ; and the merciless Brutus, far from
relenting at so moving a sight, redoubled their calamities, which he was partly the cause of. He separated
them, and deprived them of the pleasure of complaining
to each other without redress. After a cruel journey,
they arrived at the wicked fairy's, who expressed a ma-
lign joy to see the prince and young princess in a condition so worthy of creating pity in any other's breast
but her's ; however, Azira had some for Parcinus, but
durst not shew it before the fairy : ' I will (said that
' cruel queen, addressing herself to the young prince)
' have the pleasure of revenging myself on thy ingrati-
' tude ; go, instead of ascending the throne my bounty
' designed you, to the prison of the sea, where I will put
' an end to thy miserable life, by the most horrible pu-
' nishments.' ' I chuse rather the most wretched pri-
' son (replied the prince, looking on her fiercely) than
' the favours of so unjust a queen.' Which words pro-
voked her much more, who expected to have seen him
prostrate at her feet. She made him be carried away
to the appointed prison : Irolita cried on seeing him go ;
Azira could not refrain her sighs ; and all the court
groaned secretly at so cruel an order. For the fair Irolita, the queen sent her to the castle where she had been
kept so long, had her carefully guarded, and used her
as inhumanly as she was capable of.

The prince's prison was in a tower in the midst of
the sea, built on a small desert isle : there he was kept
loaded with irons, and underwent all manner of hardships. What a place was this for a prince fit to rule the
whole world ? the remembrance of Irolita was his sole.
employ ; he called on Favourable only to her assistance,
and wished a thousand times to die, to expiate the crime
he had committed : his faithful slave was put into the
same prison, but had not the satisfaction of serving his
illustrious master, who had none but rude soldiers about
him, devoted to the fairy ; who, though obedient to her,

D 2

could

could not but refpect the unhappy prince. His youth, beauty, and above all, his courage, touched them with an admiration that made them look on him as a man fuperior to all others. The prudent Mana was treated in the caftle with Irolita, in the fame manner as the faithful flave. None but Danamo's creatures came nigh the princefs, who, by her order, excited in her a frefh grief every moment, by telling her what the prince fuffered. The calamities of Parcinus made the princefs fometimes forget the remembrance of her own, and renewed her tears in a place where fhe had fo often heard that charming prince fwear to her eternal fidelity: ' Alas! (faid fhe to herfelf, why was you fo conftant, ' my dear prince; indeed, your infidelity would have ' coft me my life, but what fignified that? you would ' after that, have been happy. Danamo, who took fome time to prepare a charm of extraordinary force, fent Irolita, in the morning, two lamps one of Gold, the other of cryftal; the golden one was lighted, Danamo ordered her not to let one of thefe two lamps go out, but told her, ' She might keep which fhe pleafed lighted.' Irolita anfwered, with her natural fweetnefs, fhe fhould obey her, without fearching into the fignification of it. She carried the two lamps carefully into her clofet, and as the golden one was lighted, fhe put it not out all that day, and lighted the other the next day, and fo continued to obey the fairy. She had kept thefe lamps fifteen days, when her health began to diminifh, which fhe thought might be occafioned by her grief? but when they told her Parcinus was very ill, her piercing grief, and violent oppreffion, raifed pity in all the women about her. One night, when they were all afleep, one of them went foftly to the princefs, and feeing the cryftal lamp burning: ' What is it you do, great prin- ' cefs! (faid fhe to her) put out that fatal light, your ' health depends upon it, preferve a life fo valuable, from the cruelties of Danamo.' Alas (replied the me- ' lancholy Irolita, in a languifhing air) fhe had made ' it fo miferable, that it is a kind of a favour in the ' fairy to afford me the means of putting an end to it:
but

' but, (continued she, with an emotion that brought a
' colour in her face) whose life does that golden lamp
' prevail over ?' 'Parcinus's (replied Danamo's confi-
' dent, who spoke to the princess by her order ; for
that wicked fairy had a mind to torment her, by letting
her know how cruel her fate was. At this news the
grief of having herself taken care to put an end to
Parcinus's days, made her lay some time insensible ;
but when she came to herself, and in recovering her
senses, resumed her sorrows. ' Odious fairy (said she,
' when she had power to speak) barbarous fairy! is
' not my death sufficient to appease thy rage ? but to
' be more cruel thou must destroy, by my hands, a
' prince so dear to me, who is deserving of the tender-
' est and most perfect love ? but death, a thousand times
' more kind than thou, will shortly deliver me from
' all the mischiefs thy rage invents, against a passion
' so violent and faithful. The young princess cried
continually over the fatal lamp, on which Parcinus's
life depended, and lighted none but her own, which she
saw burn with joy, as a sacrifice she offered up to her
love and lover. All this time that unhappy prince was
tormented with punishments his courage could not
support : the fairy made the soldiers, who guarded him,
and feigned to be sensible of that illustrious prince's sorrows, tell him, ' That Irolita had consented to marry
' the prince Brutus in a few days after he was put
' into prison, and that the princess seemed very well
' content with her marriage, at all the feasts that were
' made to celebrate it ; and in short, that she was gone
' away with her husband.' This was a misfortune the
prince did not expect, and was the only one that could
be greater then his constancy. ' What, my dear, Irolita,
' are you unfaithful to me (said the sad prince) to be
' prince Brutus's ? you have only bewailed my misfor-
' tunes, and thought of putting an end to those my ten-
' derness caused you : but live happy ungreatful Iroli-
' ta, I adore you, inconstant as you are, and will die for
' my love, though not permitted the honour of dying
' for my princess.' Whilst the unfortunate Parcinus

was thus afflicting himself, and the tender Irolita was waifting her life to prolong her lover's, Danamo was affected with Azira's defpair, who died away with grief at the hardfhips of Parcinus. In fhort, the cruel fairy perceiving, that to fave her daughter's life, fhe muft pardon the prince, fuffered her to go and fee him, and to promife him all he fhould name, if he would marry her ; and at the fame time refolved to have put Irolita to death, as foon as the prince had accepted the propofi-tions. - The hopes of feeing Parcinus again; gave the melancholy Azira new life ; the queen bid her fend to Irolita for the lamp, that fhe might be fhure it did not burn ; which order feemed more cruel than all the reft to the forrowful Irolita   How great was her uneafinefs for the life of Parcinus ? ' Be not fo concerned for the ' life of that prince, (faid the women to her, who were ' about her) he is going to marry the princefs Azira, ' and it is fhe who, careful of his life, fends for the ' lamp.' The torment of jealoufy, which was wan-ting among all her misfortunes, never till after thefe words had any fhare in her calamities.   Neverthelefs Azira went to fee the prince, and offered herfelf and kingdoms to him, pretending to be ignorant that he had heard of Irolita's marriage with Brutus ; by which exam-ple fhe would have convinced him, he had carried his conftancy too far.   Parcinus, to whom nothing was valuable but his beloved Irolita, prefered his prifon and fufferings before liberty and empire.   Azira defpaired at his refufal, and her grief rendered her equally unhappy with that prince.

During this time the fairy Favourable, who till then had boafted of the infenfibility of her heart, was not able to refift the charms of a young prince in her court, who was in love with her ; and this fairy could not have refolved to liften to him, had not the pride of her foul been overcome by this violence of her paffion.   In fhort, fhe yielded to the defire of letting him know how he triumphed.   The pleafure of fpeaking to what we love, feemed then fo charming to her, and fo worthy of being defired, that approving what fhe had blamed

fo

fo much, fhe came in hafte to the Affiftance of Parcinus and the fair Irolita.

Had fhe ftaid a little longer, it would have been too late, the fatal lamp of Irolita had but fix days to burn, and the grief of the unhappy Parcinus had almoft put an end to his days. Favourable arrived at Danamo's palace, and as her power was fuperior to hers, fhe would be obeyed in fpite of the wicked fairy. The prince was fetched out of his prifon, from whence he would not ftir, till he was affured by Favourable, that the fair Irolita might ftill be his. He appeared for all his palenefs, as handfome as the day, and went with the fairy Favourable to the princefs's caftle, whofe lamp caft but a glimmering light. The dying Irolita would not confent to have it put out, till fhe was affured of the fidelity of her happy lover. No words or expreffions are lively and tender enough, to give an idea of their joy to fee each other again, Favourable made them inftantly refume their former charms, and endowed them with a long life and conftant happinefs; but for their tendernefs fhe had nought to add to that. Danamo, outrageous to fee her authority defeated, killed herfelf, leaving the fate of Azira and Brutus entirely to Irolita, who took no other revenge than marrying them both together. Parcinus was generous as conftant, accepted only of his father's kingdom, and left thofe of Danamo's to Azira. The nuptials of the prince and divine Irolita, were folemnized with great magnificence; and after having paid their acknowledgements to Favourable, and rewarded the flave, and prudent Mana, they fet out for th ir kingdom; where the prince and lovely Irolita enjoyed the hapinefs of a paffion, as tender and conftant in their profperity, as it was violent and faithful in their adverfity.

THE

THE

STORY

OF THE

PRINCESS ROSETTA.

UPON a time, there was a king and queen of a certain country, who had two fine boys, whom the queen took such care to have well bred, that they improved greatly. Her majesty was never brought to bed, but she sent to invite the fairies to her labour, and begged them to tell her her child's fortune as soon as it was born.

She became with child again, and was delivered of a daughter. so very fair, that every one who saw her was in love with her. The queen commanded the fairies to be very well treated; and when they where almost ready to take their leaves of her, she desired them not to forget their good custom, but to tell her what should happen to Rosetta (so the infant princess was called.) The fairies told her, they had left their scheme book at home, and would come another time to satisfy her.— Ah, says the queen, this does not prophesy good : you are not willing to trouble me with an unwelcome prediction ; ' speak freely I beg it of you; let me know ' the worst of her fate ; hide nothing from me,' They all desired to be excused ; and the more backward they were to tell her fortune, the more eager the queen was to know. At last the chief of them said, 'We are afraid, madam Rosetta will be the cause of a very great misfortune to her brothers, and that they will die for her somehow or other. ' This is all that we can foresee ' of the fair princess, and we are very sorry we have ' no better information to give you.' The fairies went away, and left the queen so melancholy, that the king took notice of it, and demanded the reason. She answered, ' That sitting too near the fire, she happened

to

‘ to burn all the flax on her spindle.’ ‘ Is that all (quoth
‘ the king’ :) So he goes up into the garret, and fetched
her more flax than she could spin in an hundred years.

The queen continued melancholy, and the king being inquisitive to know the cause of it, she replied,
‘ That walking near the river side, she let one of her
‘ green satin slippers fall into the water. ‘ Is that all,
(quoth the king.’) He presently set all the shoe-makers
in the kingdom to work, and brought her ten thousand
pair of green satin slippers to make up the matter. Still
she continued as melancholy as ever. He asked her the
cause of it again. She told him, ‘ That eating one day
‘ with too hasty an appetite, she chanced to swallow
‘ her wedding ring, which she had upon her finger.’
The king knowing she did not speak truth then, (for
he had locked up the ring) said to her, ‘ My dear wife,
‘ this cannot be true, for I have your ring safe under
‘ lock and key;’ and he immediately went and fetched
it. The queen finding she was caught in an untruth,
one of the foulest crimes in the world, to vindicate herself, confessed what the fairies had foretold of little Rosetta, and desired him, if he could think of any means to
prevent it, to let her know it. The king was mightily
concerned, and said to the queen, he knew no way of
preventing the destruction of their two sons, but to kill
the child while she was in her swaddling clothes. His
wife wished she might die herself first, and bid him contrive some other means to save their two boys, for she
would never consent to that.

The king and queen thinking of nothing else, studied
so many ways, that in the end they thought they had
found out one. The queen was informed that there was
an old hermit in a wood near the city, whose dwelling
was in a hollow tree, and that he was a wonderful person in matters of counsel. She therefore resolved to go
and consult him, the fairies not having told the remedy
when they predicted the evil. She rose one morning
early, mounted on a little white mule shod with gold ;
and was attended by two of her maids of honour on
horse-back, each upon a fine horse. When the queen

D 5 and

and her maids arrived at the entrance of the wood, they alighted, and walked on foot to the place where the old hermit lived in his tree. The folitaire did not like to fee women; but when he faw it was the queen, he cried, ' you are welcome, what would you have of ' me?' She then related what the fairies had foretold . her of Rofetta; and afked his advice in the cafe. He bade her fhut the princefs up in a tower, and never let her come out of it. The queen thanked him, gave him alms, and returned to tell the king her adventure.

His majefty approving of the hermit's coufel, order- ed a large tower to be built, and enclofed his daughter in it. There fhe lived: and that fhe might not be wea- ry of fo retired a life, the king, queen, and her two brothers, vifited her every day. The eldeft of them was called the great prince, and the youngeft the little prince, for diftinction fake. They loved their fifter moft dearly, for fhe was one of the beft and moft beau- tiful creatures in the world, and the leaft glance of hers was worth an hundred pounds. When fhe was fifteen years old, the great prince faid to the king, ' Papa, ' they fay that my fifter is big enough to be married: ' fhall not we go foon to her wedding?' the little prince fpoke to the fame effect to the queen; and their majef- ties amufed them with evafive anfwers, without taking notice of the marriage.

At laft the king and queen fell very ill, and died both in one day. Difmal was the ftate of the court; every one was in tears! nothing was to be feen but black coats and gowns, and nothing to be heard but tol- ling of bells. Rofetta above all wanted to be comforted, for the lofs of fo good a mother.

When the king and queen were buried, the marqui- fes and dukes of the kingdom conducted the great prince to a throne of gold and diamonds, on which he afcended, had a royal crown put upon his head, and was arrayed in robes of purple velvet, embroidered with a fun and ftars. Then the whole court fhouted, ' Long live the ' king!' and their forrow for their late majefties deaths was forgot in their joy for his prefent majefty's fucceffion.

The

The king and his brother conferring together, fpoke to this purpofe : ' Now the power is in our own hands, ' let us releafe our fifter out of the tower, wherein fhe ' has already been too long fhut up.' It was no fooner faid than done. They had only a garden to crofs, and t ey came to the tower, which was built in one corner of it, as high as it could be made ; for the late king and queen refolved fhe fhould ftay there all her life time.— Rofetta was then embroidering a robe in a frame which ftood before her ; but as foon as fhe faw her brothers, fhe rofe, and taking the king by the hand, addreffed herfelf to him in thefe words : ' good morrow, fir ; you ' are now king, and I am now your poor obedient fer- ' vant ; I beg you to let me come out of this tower, for ' I am quite tired with ftaying here.' She then burft out into a flood of tears. The king embraced her, bade her not weep, for he came there on purpofe to fetch her thence, and carry her to a fine palace. The prince's pockets were full of fweet meats, which he gave to Ro- fetta. ' Come (fays he) let us leave this filthy tower : ' do not afflict thyfelf, the king will get thee a hufband ' in a little while.'

When Rofetta faw the gardens full of flowers, fruits, and fountains, fhe was fo ravifhed that fhe could not fay a word, for fhe had never feen any thing like it before. She gazed about her as if fhe had been wild ; fometimes walked, and fometimes ftopped : fhe gathered the fruits of the trees, the flowers in the borders. Fretillion, her little dog, who was as green as a parrot, and had but one ear, danced all the way before her, and jumped and capered about as if he was as glad as his miftrefs that they were got out into the frefh air.

The company were well pleafed with Fretillion's frifking and leaping over the walks : when all of a fud- den he ran to a little wood. The princefs followed her dog, and never was woman more aftonifhed than fhe was at the fight of a huge peacock, that ftrutted as fhe approached him, and fpread out his tail. She was fo charmed with him, and thought him fo very fine, that fhe could not take her eyes off of him. The king and

prince

prince followed her, afked what fhe was fo taken with ?
fhe fhewed them the peacock, and afked what it was. —
They told her it was a bird which they fometimes eat of.
‘ How (faid fhe) are you fo cruel to kill and eat fo
‘ lovely a bird ? I here proteft to you, that I will never
‘ marry with any one but the King of the Peacocks, and
‘ when I am queen, I will hinder your eating them.’
The king was furprifed at this beyond meafure : ‘ But,
‘ fifter, (replied he) where will you find the King of
‘ the Peacocks ?’ Where you pleafe (quoth the princefs,)
‘ but I never marry any one elfe.’

Upon this the two brothers conducted her to their
palace, whither the peacock was brought, and carried
to her bed-chamber, for fhe was mightily ennamoured
of him. All the ladies who had not feen Rofetta, came
to wait upon her, and made their court; when fome
brought her comfits, others fugar-plumbs, others robes
of cloth of gold, others ribbons, others toys, others
embroidered fhoes, adorned with pearls and diamonds :
every body gave her fomething to welcome her abroad ;
and fhe was fo very obliging, courtious, and thankful for
what fhe had received at the hands of her vifitants,
that they all of them went away very well fatisfied.
While fhe was taken up with a great deal of company,
the king and the prince endeavoured to find out the
King of the Peacocks, if there was any fuch monarch
in the world. They thought it convenient to have their
fifter’s picture drawn, to fhew to the prince with the
broad tail, if they fhould happen to light upon him :
and it was indeed drawn fo beautifully, that it wanted
fpeech only to be as lovely as the original. When that
was done, the two brothers told the princefs, that fince
fhe would marry nobody but the King of the Peacocks,
they would go together all over the world in fearch of
him. If we find him, we will bring him to you with
joy ; in the mean time do you take care of our kingdom
till we return.

Rofetta thanked them for the trouble they took for
her fake, and affured them fhe would carefully govern
the kingdom in their abfence ; during which all her delight

light would he in the lovely Peacock in her chamber, and the tricks of the little Fretillion. So they bade each other adieu, not without some showers of tears at parting.

As they said, they did : the king and prince rambled up and down, asking every where for the King of the Peacocks : nobody knew him. They went so far, so very far, that nobody ever went farther.

They arrived at the kingdom of Locusts, and never saw the like before, there was such buzzing, that his majesty was afraid of losing his hearing. He asked one of them, who looked to be a locust of parts, if he could tell where he might find the King of the Peacocks?— ' Sir, (replied the insect) his kingdom is thirty thousand ' leagues off: you have gone out of your way to it.' ' How do you know that ? (says the king) Oh, sir, ' (quoth the Locust) we know you very well, for we ' come every year to spend two or three months in your ' gardens.' Immediately the king and his brother became acquainted with the Locust, and many civil things passed between them. They dined together, and his majesty and highness took delight in viewing the curiosities of the country, where the least leaf on a tree was worth a guinea. When they had been kindly treated by the host, they proceeded on their journey ; and knowing the way to the place they were bound to, it was not long before they arrived at it. The trees were all loaded with Peacocks, and the number of them so great, that their chuckling might be heard two leagues off. Says the king to his brother , ' If the King of the Peacocks should be a ' Peacock himself, how can our sister pretend to have ' him for a husband ? we should be made to consent ' to it ; and what a fine alliance will she engage us in ! ' besides, what an honour it will be to us to have a little ' Pea chicken for our nephew !' The prince was as much concerned about it as the king. ' It is a wretched fan- ' cy of her's (quoth he) who could put it into her head, ' that there was such a creature upon the earth as the ' King of the Peacocks?' When they arrived at the capital city they saw that it was full of men and women,
but

but that their clothes were all made of Peacocks feathers which they met with wherever they came. They found the king taking the air in a rich little coach of gold and diamonds. This monarch was so handsome, that the king and prince were charmed with him. His hair was fair, curled and long; his complexion fair also; and on his head he wore a crown made of a peacock's tail. When he espied them, he imagined by their dress that they were strangers; and to inform himself concerning them, stopped his coach, and ordered them to be called to him.

The king and prince approached him, made him a very low bow, saying, 'Sir, we are come from a far country, to shew to you a lovely picture:' and then pulled out that of their sister, which they carried in a case.— When the King of the Peacocks saw it, ' I do not believe (said he) ' there is so beautiful a lady in the universe.' The king answered, 'She is a hundred times handsomer ' than her picture. ' You banter me (quoth the mo- ' narch of the fine tailed nation.') The prince then took his brother's part. ' Sir (said he) my brother is a ' king as well as yourself; he is called the king, and I am ' called the prince; our sister, whose picture you see ' here, is named Rosetta. We are come to ask you if ' you will marry her: she is handsome and discreet, ' and we will give you with her a bushel of crowns of ' gold. ' Say you so (quoth the King of the Peacocks) ' I will marry her with all my heart: but be you shure ' that she is as handsome as her picture, for otherwise ' you shall be both put to death.' Agreed (replied Ro- ' setta's two brothers.') ' Then here (says the king to ' the captain of his guards) put these two persons into ' prison; they shall remain there till the princess arrives. The princes obeyed, without making any difficulty of it, for they knew Rosetta was handsomer than her portrait.

During their confinement they were treated to a wonder: the king came often to visit them, and hung Rosetta's picture up in his palace, being so enamoured with it, that he could not sleep night nor day, the image

of

of the fair lady running always in his mind. The king
and the prince wrote from their prison to the princess
by the post, to come away with all speed, for the King
of the Peacocks expected her. They did not let her
know they were prisoners, for fear of troubling her too
much.

  When she received the letter, she was so overjoyed
she could hardly contain herself. She told every body
she met, the King of the Peacocks was found, and she
was to marry him. Bonfires were presenly lighted
through all the city : the cannon discharged ; the choisest
viands and sweet-meats were devoured by cart loads;
and the princess for three days kept open house, treating
all her guests with the richest wines. After which she
bestowed her fine babies on her best friends, and, com-
mitting the government to the oldest and wisest persons
of the city, recommending to them to have a care of
the state, to spend nothing, but to save all they could for
the king ; packed up her baggage, and departed, leaving
her Peacock behind her, having given the regents a strict
charge to be careful of him. Her dog Fretrillion, her
nurse, and foster-sister, were the only companions of
her voyage, for she went by sea. She carried with her
the bushel of crowns of gold that were to be her portion,
and change of suits sufficient to last her ten years, at
two suits a day. She did nothing but sing and dance :
and her nurse was always inquiring of the master of the
vessel, whether they were not come near the kingdom
of the Peacocks ? he still answered, ' No, no.' She asked
him still, ' Are we now come ?' ' Have a little patience
' good woman (quoth the tar) we shall arrive in good
' time.' ' Are we come now ? (says the nurse again.')
' Yes, you are come (replied the mariner.') And when
he had said it, she drew up near him, seated herself
down by him, and spoke to him thus: ' It is now in thy
' power to make thyself as rich as thou pleasest ; do as
' I would have thee, and thou shalt have as much money
' as thou wilt.' He answered, ' What must I do for
' it ?' ' I will give thee thy pocket full of guineas (quoth
she,') ' Will you so, says the mariner, I desire no better
                                                    sport

' fport ; let us finger them as foon as you pleafe', The
nurfe went on, ' What I require of you in return is, that
' this night, when the princefs is a fleep, thou wilt help me
' to throw her into the fea ; when fhe is drowned, I
' will drefs my daughter up in her cloaths, and we will
' carry her to the King of the Peacocks, who will marry
' her; and for thy reward thou fhalt have a diamond
' bracelet.

The mariner was furprifed at the nurfe's cruel propofal. ' It is a pity (faid he) to drown fuch a fair prin-
' cefs.' But the wicked woman cured his fcruples with
a bottle or two of wine, and he agreed to ferve her.

About midnight, the princefs being faft a fleep, with
her little dog Fretrillion by her, the nurfe went to the
mariner, and made him enter Rofetta's cabin : They
took her up, bed and all, and threw her into the fea,
her fofter-fifter lending her helping hand. The princefs did not wake with the ftir they made, nor with the
blow of the fall; but what was happy for her, the feathers
of her bed were phœnix's, which are very rare, and
have that good quality, they never fink, fo Rofetta
fwam upon her bed as fafely, and as much at her eafe,
as if fhe had been in the veffel. The water by degrees
however wetted the matting firft, and then the bed and
blankets. The princefs feeling the wet about her,
was at firft a little alarmed, but was quiekly recoveied.

Her turning herfelf from one fide to the other waked
Fretillion, who had an excellent nofe, and fmelt the foles
and flounders that were near him : He fell a barking, fo
that it waked all the other fifh, who began to fwim
about them. The great fifh ran their heads againft the
princefs's bed, which being faftened to nothing, was
toffed to and fro like a fhuttle-cock. My lady wondered
what was the matter. ' How, (fays fhe) does our vef-
' fel dance fo upon the water ? I never lay fo uneafy
' in my life as I have done to night.' Fretillion in
the mean while barked at the fifh fo loudly, that the
nurfe and mariner heard him. 'That rogue of a dog
(faid fhe) ' is, I warrant ye, drinking our health
' with his miftrefs; let us not mind them, but make
to ·

' to port as fast as we can:' And it was not long before they arrived at the King of the Peacock's capital.

The monarch ordered a hundred coaches, drawn by all sorts of rare beasts to meet the princess at the sea side. Some were drawn by lions, some by bears, some by stags, wolves, horses, oxen, asses, eagles, and peacocks. The coach which Rosetta was to ride in, was drawn by six blue monkeys, who capered and danced, and played a thousand pretty tricks: Their harness was made of crimson velvet, with plates of gold. The king commanded sixty young virgins to wait upon her at her arrival.—They were dressed in all sorts of colours; and silver and gold were the least things about them.

The nurse had taken a great deal of pains to set off her daughter; she dressed her head with Rosetta's diamonds, and clothed her in her finest robes. But with all her finery she was exceeding ugly: Her hair was black and greasy; her eyes squinted; she was hump-backed, and of such an ill humour, that she was always a scolding.

When the King of the Peacock's servant saw her come out of the vessel, they were struck dumb with astonishment. ' Who is here (quoth she) What, are you all ' fast asleep? Go, go, ye rascals, fetch me something ' to eat, or I will have you all hanged.' They were startled at her threats, and said one to another, ' What ' filthy beast is come amongst us; she is as ill natured ' as she is ugly: Our king is finely helped up in a wife: ' there was no need of sending to the end of the world ' for such a lady as this is.' The pretended princess continued her airs, and for little or nothing fell foul upon her attendants with her tongue and fist.

Her equipage being very great, she could not go fast along. She lolled in her coach like a queen; but the peacocks, who had posted themselves on the trees thereabouts, to salute her, as she passed by, intending to welcome her with shouts of ' Long live the fair queen ' Rosetta,' when they saw this fair creature, cried out, ' Fie, fie, how ugly she is!' The jade, enraged at them bid her guards kill those rascally peacocks; dare they affront and rail at me! the peacocks laughed at her and flew away.

The

The rogue of a mariner, who saw what paſſed, whiſ-pered the nurſe, ' Mother we are in a ſorry condition: ' your daughter ſhould have been a little handſomer.' She replied, ' Hold your tongue, you blockhead, or you ' will ſpoil all.

· The king receiving intimation that the princeſs ap-proached ; ' Well ſaid he to his courtiers, have the two ' brothers told me truth ? is ſhe handſomer than her ' picture.' They anſwered, ' It were to be wiſhed, ſir, ' that ſhe would prove as handſome.' ' I deſire no ' more, ſays the king; let us go and ſee what ſhe is :' for by this time the mock princeſs and her train were arrived in the great court in the palace, and the noiſe was ſuch, that he could not diſtinguiſh what they ſaid, only he could hear ſome of the crowd that were neareſt to him cry, ' Out upon her, how ugly ſhe is!' The king thought they ſpoke it of ſome dwarf or monkey that ſhe had brought along with her, for he could not imagine that it was ſhe herſelf they ſaid this of.

Roſetta's picture was carried before the king at the end of a long ſtaff, and his majeſty followed it gravely with his barons, his peacocks, and the ambaſſadors of the ſeveral kingdoms reſident in his court. The king was very impatient to ſee his dear Roſetta ; but when he ſaw her ladyſhip, it was feared he would drop down dead in the place : He fell in the moſt terrible paſſion that ever was ſeen ; tore his garments, and would not come near her, being afraid of her as if ſhe had been a fiend, and not a human creature.

' Have theſe two villains, whom I have in priſon (ſaid he) ' had the impudence to make a jeſt of me ' and propoſe a baboon to me for a wife ? they ſhall ' die; go take that gipſey, her nurſe, and he that ' brought them, thr w them into the dungeon in my ' great tower ; I will make examples of them all.'

In the mean time, the king and his brother, who were priſoners, hearing their ſiſter was arrived, and was ma-king her public entry, had dreſſed themſelves as fine as they could to receive her : but, inſtead of opening their priſon doors to ſet them at liberty, the gaoler came with

twenty.

twenty foldiers, and caried them down into a dark dungeon, which was full of naftinefs and vermin, and where they ftood up to their necks in water. Nothing can be imagined more dreadful to perfons of their rank. ‘ Alas (faid they to each other) it is an unhappy wed-‘ ding day to us !’ What could be the caufe of their fuf-ferings they could not conceive, only they faw their death was refolved on, and were both in a moft deplorable ftate of defpair. Three days paft over their heads, and they heard no tidings of any thing. At laft the King of the Peacocks came, and railed at them thro’ a hole. You have ufurped the title of king and prince to deceive me, and impofe your fifter on me; but you are all a company of rafcals, who do not deferve the water you drink: I fhall take a courfe with you: your judges are preparing for your trial, and the rope is making that is to hang you. ‘ King of the Peacocks, (replied the king in a rage) do not make fo much hafte, ‘ you may repent it one time or other : I am a king ‘ as well as yourfelf ; I have a large kingdom royal ‘ robes, crowns and money in good ftore. You are ‘ merry fure, when you talk of hanging us : have we ‘ ftolen any thing from you ?

When the king heard him fpeak with fo much refolu-tion, he could not tell what to do: he had almoft a mind to releafe them, and fend them home with their fifter ; but one of his favourites (a true court flatterer) confirmed him in his defign to have them tied up ; otherwife, he faid, every body would fcorn him, to be tricked by fuch forry fellows. He then fwore he would never forgive them, and ordered that they fhould be brought to a trial ; which did not laft long, for there was no need of much proof : the portrait of the real Rofetta was produced, as alfo the perfon of the counterfeit. The impofture was plain : fo the two princes were con-demned to be beheaded as cheats, for having promifed the king a beautiful princefs, and inftead of fuch a one, prefented him with an ugly wench, hardly fit for his groom.

The

The judges went in great solemnity to the prison, to pronounce the princes sentence; who cried out, they had not put any trick upon him; that their sister was a princess, and as bright as the day; that there must be some mistake in the matter; and desired respite of execution for seven days, in which time their innocence might be made appear. The King of the Peacocks, who was mightily enraged at them, could hardly be persuaded to favour them so far; but at last he was prevailed with to spare their lives so long.

While things went on thus at court, the poor princess Rosetta was in a miserable condition. As soon as day broke, she was amazed to find herself in the middle of the sea, and Fretillion in no less amazement than his mistress. She wept, and wept as if she meant to swell the ocean with her tears. The fish who beheld them, pitied the sorowful princess. She knew not what to do, nor what to think. 'Certainly (said she to herself) I 'was flung here by the King of the Peacock's order; 'he repents of marrying me, and to get rid of me would 'have me drowned. He is a strange sort of a man 'surely, for I should have loved him so well, and we 'should have lived so comfortably together?, She then fell a weeping again more than ever, for she could not help loving him.

Two days she remained floating upon the sea, soaked to the very bone, numbed with cold, and almost ready to give up the ghost; and indeed, had it not been for the company of her Fretillion, she had died a hundred times in those two days, if it had been possible. She was very hungry; but she took up oysters as many as she could, and swallowed them. Fretillion did not love them, yet as he must eat them or starve, it brought his stomach too a little. When night came, Rosetta's fears increased; and quoth she to her dog, ' Bark, Fre- 'tillion, least the fish eat us.' He barked all night, and the current drove the princess's bed on shore, near an old man's house, who lived alone in a little cottage, where nobody ever came to see him. He was very poor, and did not mind worldly goods, provided he had ease
and

and suſtenance. When he heard Fretrillion bark he was surprised, and could not tell whether he was awake or asleep, there being no dogs in his neighbourhood.—He imagined that some travellers were got out of their way, and came out of his hut with a charitable intention to put them into it. On a sudden he espied the princess and Fretrillion swimming on the sea ; and the princess seeing him, held up her hand, crying out. ‘ Help me ‘ father, or we shall perish : I have languished already ‘ these two days.’

When he heard her make that pitiful moan, he was touched to the heart with compaſſion, ran into his house to fetch out a long pole with a crook at the end, to pull the bed ashore, and went into the sea up to his chin to hawl her out, which, not without much danger and difficulty, he effected. Rosetta and Fretrillion both rejoiced when they set foot on dry ground. She thanked the good man for affiſting her, and wrapped herself up in her coverlid : then, barefoot as she was, she walked to his cottage, where he lighted a fire of dry leaves, and took his late wife's bed-gown, with some clean shoes and stockings, to clothe the princess ; who, thus dreſſed like a country girl, looked as fair as the morning, and Fretrillion leaped about to divert her.

And when the perils of the deep are o'er,
With food supply'd the fainting fair ashore ;
None ever such an useful creature knew,
Or dog so serviceable and so true.
Rosetta, *who so much had suffered, spar'd*
The traitors, fearful of their crime's reward.
Learn ye, who have been injur'd, to forgive
Like her, and to restrain your vengeance strive :
Besides that fortune, now your friend, may change,
'Tis greater to forgive, than to revenge.

The good old man perceived that Rosetta was a lady of quality, for the coverlid of her bed was cloth of gold and silver, and her quilt of satin. He begged her to tell him her adventures, and promised not to say a

6   word

word, if she exacted silence from him. To satisfy him,
she told him the whole story from one end to the other,
ending her relation with tears; for she still believed that
the king of the Peacocks had ordered her to be drowned.
' What shall I get for you, that you may eat? (quoth
the old man) so great a princess as you must have been
' must have been used to dainties; and as for me, I
' have nothing but my brown bread and turnips, which
' will be but a sorry meal for your highness; if you
' would give me leave I will go and tell the King of the
' Peacocks that you are here; for certainly, as soon as
' he sees you, he will marry you.' 'Ah! (replied Ro-
' setta) he is a rogue, he would have me drowned; but
' if you have a little basket, tie it about my dog's neck,
' and he will be more unfortunate than ever I knew
' him, if he does not fetch us some provisions.' The
old man brought out a basket, and gave it the princess,
who tied it about Fretillion's neck, saying, ' Go, sirah,
' to the best pot in the city, and bring me what is in it.'
Fretillion ran to the town, and the king's pot being the
best, went strait to the kitchen royal, opened the pot,
and took out what was within it, and returned to his
mistress. Rosetta patted him on the back, and bade
him go back and do his office again. Fretillion retur-
n d a second time, so loaded with bread and wine,
fruits and sweet-meats, that he could hardly lug them
along. When the King of the Peacocks called for his
dinner the cook examining the pot which was over
the fire, found there was nothing in it, and the desert
was also missing. The servants of the household stared
upon one another, and could not guess how it was gone.
The King fell into a violent passion: however, he was
forced to go without his dinner. ' Well, (said he) let
' me have something roasted for supper, or you shall
pay for it severely.' Supper-time being come, says
the princess to Fretillion, ' Go to town, and fetch me
' the best thing out of the best kitchen there.' The dog
who had been taught to fetch and carry, did as his mistress commanded him; and knowing no kitchen better
than the king's, went thither, entered it softly, and very
                                        dextrously

dextroufly carried off the roaft meat. He returned to the princefs with his bafket full; and fhe commanding him again to do his office, he went to the palace again, and brought away the defert a fecond time.

The King having no dinner, had a good ftomach to his fupper, and ordered it to be ready early; but there was nothing for him, which threw him into a greater rage than before. He raved and ftormed, but all to no purpofe; the roafted meat was gone, and he was compelled to go to bed fupperlefs. He was ferved the fame trick the next day at dinner and fupper: fo that his majefty lived three days without eating or drinking: for whenever he fat down, the meat was always miffing. The chief favourite and minifter, who was concerned for the health of the King, hid himfelf in a little corner of the kitchen, and kept his eye upon the pot that was over the fire. He had not ftayed there long, before, to his great furprife, he faw a little green dog with one ear enter foftly, open the pot, take out the meat, and put it into his bafket, he followed, to fee where he went; the dog ran directly to his miftrefs at the old man's houfe. The favourite returned to court, and told the King what he had feen, and that both his roaft meat and boiled meat was every day carried to a poor peafant's houfe. The King was amazed at it, and commanded the country man to be brought before him. The prime minifter took fome ferjeants with him, and away they went to the peafant's houfe, where they found the princefs and the old man at dinner, eating his majefty's boiled and roaft very contentedly. The favourite bade the ferjeants apprehend them: fo Rofetta, the old man and Fretillion, were bound and led away to the palace.

When they arrived there, word was brought to the King; who anfwered, to-morrow is the laft day that thefe two cheats have to live; let the thief who robbed me of my dinner die with them. He then entered the hall of juftice to try the criminals; the old man fell upon his knees, and promifed to confefs all, if he would fpare his life. While he was fpeaking the king looked upon the fair princefs, and pitied her when he faw her weep: but when the old man declared that fhe was the princefs Rofetta, whom the wicked nurfe and mariner

had

had thrown into the fea : though the King was faint e-
nough with three days fafting, he gave three leaps for
joy, that fhewed his majefty could cut a caper with the
nimbleft of them. He ran to the princefs, unbound
her, embraced her, and faid he loved her dearly.

He prefently gave orders to bring forth the princes
who imagined it was to their execution, held down their
heads like condemned men. The nurfe and her daught. r
were alfo fent for. When they all met together, they
all knew one another. The princefs threw her arms
about her brothers necks: the nurfe and mariner begged
pardon upon their knees. The king and the princefs
were fo overjoyed, that they forgave them. The good
old countryman was liberally rewarded, and had an
apartment in the palace, where he lived all his life-time
afterwards. The King of the Peacocks did his utmoft
to make the princes amends for their fufferings. The
nurfe reftored Rofetta her rich robes and the bufhel of
crowns of gold. The nuptial feftival lafted fifteen days;
every one was pleafed, not excepting even Fretillion,
who would eat nothing for the future but the wings of
partridges.

THE MORAL.

Heaven is our guard, and innocence its care,
Nor need the juft the worft of dangers fear ;
It pities the defencelefs virgin's grief,
And fends her, when fhe calls, help and relief;
It arms the fureft fuccour and the beft,
Delivers and revenges the diftrefs'd.

When fair Rofetta on the waves was toft,
What hope had fhe to reach the diftant coaft ?
Who that had heard the billows round her roar
Could think fhe ever could have gain'd the fhore ?
Who would not have believ'd her lovely flefh
Would be fome hungry whale's delicious difh ?

Soft pity muft have melted all his frame,
To view the dangers of the floating dame.
Heav'n heard her cries, or foon fhe'd been a prey
To death and the fell monfters of the fea.
His part her little dog Fretillion play'd,
Who fnapt the finny foes to fave the maid.

THE

CURIOUS STORY

OF THE

WHITE MOUSE.

IN the kingdom of Bonbobbin, which, by the Chinese annals appears to have flourished twenty thousand years ago, there reigned a prince, endowed with every accomplishment which generally distinguishes the sons of kings. His beauty was brighter than the sun. The sun, to which he was nearly related, would sometimes stop his course, in order to look down and admire him.

His mind was not less perfect than his body; he knew all things without having ever read; philosophers, poets, and historians submitted their works to his decision: and so penetrating was he, that he could tell the merit of a book, by looking on the cover. He made epick poems, tragedies, and pastorals, with surprising facility; song, epigram or rebus, was all one to him; though, it is observed he could never finish an acrostick. In short, the fairy who precided at his birth, had endowed him with almost every perfection, or what was just the same, his subjects were ready to acknowledge he possessed them all; and, for his own part, he knew nothing to the contrary. A prince so accomplished, received a name suitable to his merit: and he was called Bonbenin-bonbob-

E   bin

bin-bonbobbinet, which fignifies enlightener of the fun.

As he was very powerful, and yet unmarried, all the neighbouring kings earneftly fought his alliance. Each fent his daughter, dreffed out in the moft magnificent manner, and with the moft fumptuous retinue imaginable, in order to allure the prince ; fo that, at one time, there were feen at his court, not lefs than feven hundred foreign princeffes, of exquifite fentiment and beauty, each alone fufficient to make feven hundred ordinary men happy.

Diftracted in fuch a variety, the generous Bonbenin, had he not been obliged by the laws of the empire to make choice of one, would very willingly have married them all, for none underftood gallantry better. He fpent numberlefs hours of folicitude, in endeavouring to determine whom he fhould chufe; one lady was poffeffed of every perfection, but he difliked her eyebrows ; another was brighter than the morning ftar, but he difapproved of her fong whang ; a third did not lay white enough on her cheeks : and the fourth did not fufficiently blacken her nails. At laft, after numberlefs difappointments on the one fide and the other, he made choice of the incomparable Nanhoa, queen of the fcarlet dragons.

The preparations for the royal nuptials, or the envy of the difappointed ladies, needs no defcription ; both the one and the other were as great as they could be.—— The beautiful princefs was conducted, amidft admiring multitudes to the royal couch, where, after being divefted of every incumbering ornament, he came more chearful than the morning ; and, printing on her lips a burning kifs, the attendants took this as a proper fignal to withdraw.

Perhaps I ought to have mentioned, in the beginning, that among feveral other qualifications, the prince was fond of collecting and breeding mice, which being a harmlefs paftime, none of his councellors thought proper to diffuade him from ; he therefore kept a great variety of thefe pretty little animals, in the moft beautiful cages,
enriched

enriched with diamonds, rubies, emeralds, pearls, and other precious stones; thus he innocently spent four hours each day in contemplating their innocent little pastimes.

But, to proceed—The Prince and princess were now retired to repose; and though night and secrecy had drawn the curtain, yet delicacy retarded those enjoyments which passion presented to their view. The prince happened to look towards the outside of the bed, perceived one of the most beautiful animals in the world, a white mouse with green eyes, playing about the floor, and performing a hundred pretty tricks. He was already master of blue mice, red mice, and mice with green eyes, was what he long endeavoured to possess: wherefore, leaping from bed, with the utmost impatience and agility, the youthful prince attempted to seize the little charmer; but it was fled in a moment; for, alas! the mouse was sent by a discontented princess, and was itself a fairy.

It is impossible to describe the agony of the prince upon this occasion. He sought round and round every part of the room, even the bed where the princess lay was not exempt from the inquiry: he turned the princess on one side and the other, stripped her quite naked, but no mouse was to be found; the princess herself was kind enough to assist, but still to no purpose.

‘ Alas, (cried the young prince in an agony) how un-
‘ happy am I to be thus disappointed ? never sure was
‘ so beautiful an animal seen ; I would give half my
‘ kingdom and my princess to him that would find it.’
The princess, though not much pleased with the latter part of his offer, endeavoured to comfort him as well as she could : she let him know that he had a hundred mice, already, which ought to be at least sufficient to satisfy any philosopher like him. Though none of them had green eyes, yet he should learn to thank heaven that they had eyes. She told him (for she was a profound moralist) that incurable evils must be borne, and that useless lamentations were vain, and that man was born to misfortunes: she even entreated him to return to bed, and she would endeavour to lull him on her bosom to

E 2   repose ;

repose : but still the prince continued inconsolable ; and, regarded her with a stern air, for which his family was remarkable ; he vowed never to sleep in a royal palace or indulge himself in the innocent pleasures of matrimony, till he had found the mouse with the green eyes.

When morning came, he published an edict, offering half his kingdom, and his princess, to that person who should catch and bring him the white mouse with green eyes.

The edict was scarcely published, when all the traps in the kingdom were baited with cheese : numberless mice were taken and destroyed : but still the much wished for mouse was not among the number. The privy council were assembled more than once to give their advice ; but all their deliberations came to nothing : even tho' there were two complete vermin killers, and three professed rat-catchers of the number. Frequent addresses, as is usual on extraordinary occasions, were sent from all parts of the empire ; but though these promised well, though in them he received an assurance, that his faithful subjects would assist in his search, with their lives and fortunes, yet, with all their loyalty they failed, when the time came that the mouse was to be caught.—

The prince, therefore, was resolved to go himself in search, determined never to lay two nights in one place, till he had found what he sought for. Thus quitting his palace, without attendants, he set out upon his journey, and travelled through many a desert, and crossed many a river, high over hills, and down among vales, still restless, still inquiring wherever he came : but no white mouse was to be found.

As one day, fatigued with his journey, he was shading himself, from the heat of the mid-day sun, under the arching branches of a banana tree, meditating on the object of his pursuit, he perceived an old woman hideously deformed, approaching him : by her stoop and the wrinkles of her visage, she seemed at least five hundred years old ; and the spotted toad was not more freckled than was her skin. 'Ah? prince Bonbenin-bonbobbin-
'bonbobinet

' bonbobinet (cried the creature) what has led you so
' many thousand miles from your own kingdom?
' what is it you look for, and what induces you to travel
' into the kingdom of the emmits?' The prince, who
was excessively complaisant, told her the whole story
three times over, for she was was hard of hearing.—
' well said the old fairy, (for such she was) I promise to
' put you in possession of the White Mouse, with green
' eyes, and that immediately too, upon one condition.
' One condition (continued the prince in a rapture)
' name a thousand; I shall undergo them all with plea-
' sure.' ' Nay (interrupted the old fairy) I ask but one,
' and that not very mortifying neither; it is only that
' you instantly consent to marry me.' It is impossible
to express the prince's confusion at this demand: he
loved the mouse, but he detested the bride; he hesita-
ted; he desired time to think on the proposal. He would
have been glad to consult his friends on such an occasion. ' Nay, nay, cried the odious fairy, if you demur,
' I retract my promise; I do not desire to force my fa-
' vors on any man. Here, you my attendant, (cried
she, stamping with her foot) let my machine be driven up:
' Barbacela, queen of Emmets, is not used to contemp-
' tuous treatment.' She had no sooner spoken than
her fiery chariot appeared in the air, drawn by two
snails; and she was just going to step in, when the prince
reflected, that now or never was the time to be in possession of the white mouse; and quite forgetting his law-
ful princess, Nanhoa, falling on his knees, he implored
forgiveness for having rashly rejected so much beauty.
This well-timed compliment instantly appeased the angry fairy. She affected an hideous leer of approbation,
and taking the young prince by the hand, conducted
him to a neighbouring church, where they were married together in a moment. As soon as the ceremony
was performed, the prince who was to the last degree
desirous of seeing his favourite mouse, reminded the
bride of her promise. ' To confess a truth, my prince
(cried she) I myself am that very white mouse you saw
' on your wedding night in the royal apartment. I

now

' now therefore give you your choice, whether you would
' have me a mouse by day, and a woman by night, or
' a mouse by night, and a woman by day.' Though
the prince was an excellent casuist, he was quite at a
loss how to determine; but at last thought it most prudent to have recourse to a blue cat, that had followed
him from his own dominions, and frequently amused
him with its conversation, and assisted him with its advice: in fact this cat was no other than the faithful
princess Nanhoa herself, who had shared with him all
his hardships in this disguise.

By her instructions he was determined in his choice;
and, returning to the old fairy, prudently observed,
that, as she must have been sensible he had married her
only for the sake of what she had, and not for her person-
al qualifications, he thought it would, for several reasons,
be most convenient, if she continued a woman by day,
and appeared a mouse by night.

The old fairy was a good deal mortified at her husband's want of gallantry, though she was reluctantly o-
bliged to comply: the day was therefore spent in the
most polite amusement, the gentlemen talked, the
ladies laughed, and were angry. At last the happy night
drew near; the blue cat still stuck by the side of its master, and even followed him to the bridal apartment.—
Barbacela entered the chamber, wearing a train fifteen yards long, supported by porcupines, and all over
beset with jewels, which served to render her more detes-
table. She was just stepping into bed to the prince,
forgetting her promise, when he insisted upon seeing
her in the shape of a mouse. She had promised, and no
fairy can break her word; wherefore assuming the figure of the most beautiful mouse in the world, she skip-
ped and played about with an infinity of amusement.
The prince in an agony of rapture, was desirous of seeing his pretty playfellow move a slow dance about the
floor to his own singing; he began to sing, and the
mouse immediately to perform with the most perfect
knowledge of time, and the finest grace and greatest gra-
vity imaginable; it only began, for Nanhoa, who had
                                                        long

long waited for the opportunity, in the shape of a cat, flew upon it instantly, without remorse, and eating it up in the hundredth part of a moment, broke the charm, and then resumed her natural figure.

The prince now found that he had all along been under the power of enchantment; that his passion for the White Mouse was entirely fictious, and not the genuine complexion of his soul: he now saw, that his earnestness after mice was an illiberal amusement, and much more becoming a rat-catcher than a prince. All his meannesses now stared him in the face; he begged the princess's pardon an hundred times. The princess very readily forgave him; and both returned to their palace in Banbobbin, lived very happily together, and reigned many years, with all that wisdom, which by the story, they appear to have been possessed of. Perfectly convinced by their former adventures, that they who place their affections on trifles at first for amusement, will find those trifles at last become their most serious concern.

THE

STORY

OF

PRINCESS VERENATA.

IT happened upon a time, there was a certain king and queen, who had several children, but they all died; and the king and queen were so mightily troubled at it, that never any body could be more so. Their coffers were all full, and they wanted only children to leave their treasures to. Five years were past since the queen had a child, and all the world believed she would have no more, because she afflicted herself too much for those pretty princes which she had buried.

But at last she was with child, and all her thoughts, night and day, were what she should do to preserve the royal infant when it was born, what name she should give it, what clothes, what babies, and play-things provide for it.

Proclamation was made, and orders set up in all places, that the best nurses in the kingdom should come to court, that the queen might chuse one out of them to nurse the expected baby. Immediately the good women came from all quarters: the court was full of nurses, with their little children in their arms. The queen being one day walking to take the air in a neighbouring wood, and the king with her, she sat down to rest herself, and said to his majesty, 'Sir, pray give orders 'that all those nurses be brought hither, that we may 'make choice of one of them, for all the cows we have 'will not yield milk enough to make pap for the children 'they have brought with them.' 'Very well, my dear (replied the king') and streight he commanded that the nurses should come to them. They accordingly came, one after another, and made each a fine courtsy to their majesties. Then they stood along in a row, and the king and queen surveyed them in general first, and afterwards in particular; they examined their fresh complexions, their white teeth, and their breast full of milk. Among the rest came an ugly jade, drawn in a weel-barrow, by two nasty dwarfs: she was a cripple, and so crooked that her chin and knees almost met.— She had a great wen in her face? she squinted, and her skin was as black as ink : she held something in her arms like a little infant monkey, to which she gave suck, and spake a jargon that nobody understood. She approached their majesties in her turn to offer her service, but the queen bid her be gone; 'Get ye hence you filthy
beast

' beaft ! (quoth her majefty ;) what put it into your head
' of fuch a creature as thou art to come hither ? if thou
' doft not get thee away inftantly, I fhall order thee to
' be riven after another manner.' The beldam mut-
tered to herfelf, and retreated to an old tree, where fhe
lay in a crevice of the trunk and faw all that paffed.—
The queen thinking no more of her, chofe a handfome
young woman to be her nurfe ; but as foon as fhe had
named her, a horrible fnake, which lay in the grafs,
ftung her in the foot, and fhe fell down as if fhe had
been dead. The queen was very forry for the accident,
and made choice of another. She had no fooner done it,
but an eagle, which flew over the nurfe's head with a
huge turtle in her claws dropped it on the woman's
head, and broke it in pieces as if it had been glafs. The
queen was more concerned at this accident than the o-
ther ; yet fhe chofe a third nurfe for the child that was to
be born ; and this woman running too haftily towards
her, fell down againft the ftump of a tree, and ftruck
her eye out. ' Alas ! (fays her majefty) I fee this is an
' unfortunate day ; I cannot pitch upon a nurfe, but
' prefently fome mifchief comes to her : let a furgeon
' be fent for to look after them.' So fhe arofe from
her fear, and was returning to the palace, when fhe
heard fomebody laugh aloud ; and turning back, fhe
efpied the old deformed beldam behind her, like a ba
·boon's mate with her young ape in a wheel-barrow. —.
She laughed at the whole company, and at the queen
in particular : which fo enraged her majefty, that fhe
would have fallen upon and beaten her, very much
fufpecting that fhe had been the caufe of the mifchiefs
that had befallen the nurfes. But the jade ftruck thrice
with her wand, and the dwarfs were immediately chan-
·ged into dragons, the weel-barrow into a chariot of fire,
and away fhe flew into the air, threatning what fhe
would do to all of them, and making dreadful cries.—
' Alas, (faid the king) we are undone ! it is the fairy
' ·Caraboffa ; the wretch has hated me ever fince I was
' a little boy, for playing her a trick once, and throwing

E 5   fome

. fome brimftone into her porridge : fhe vowed to be
. . revenged, and has from that time taken all opportuni-
. ties to exercife her vengeance upon me.' The queen
wept, and replied, 'Had I known who fhe was, fir,
' I had given her good words, and endeavoured to have
' m de her my friend. This misfortune will certainly
' be the death of me.' When the king faw fhe grieved
fo much about it : he ftrove to comfort her, though he
wanted comfort himfelf. ' Come, my dear (fays the
, monarch) let us go and confult our council upon the
' matter.' He then took her by the arm, and held her
up as fhe walked home, for fhe trembled ftill at the
thoughts of the danger fhe was in from Caraboffa's revenge.

. When their majefties returned to their palace, they
fummoned their chief counfellors to attend them in their
chamber. The doors and windows were fhut very clofe
that they might not be overheard ; and it was gravely
refolved, that all the fairies a thoufand leagues about
fhould be invited to the queen's labour. Couriers
were difpatched, and very civil letters written to the
fairy ladies to defire them to come to her majefty's crying-
out, and to keep the matter fecret, for fear Caraboffa
fhould hear of it. To fatisfy them for their trouble,
each of them was promifed a waiftcoat of blue velvet,
a petticoat of crimfon, fome pink fatin, flippers of the
fame colour, fome gilded fciffars, and a needle-cafe full
of fine needles.

As foon as the meffengers were departed, the queen
and her maids fet to work to provide the things that
were promifed to be given the fairies. She knew feveral, but there came only five. They arrived in the
very moment that the queen was brought to bed of a
princefs. The fairies would each give her a bleffing:
one endowed her with perfect beauty ; another with an
infinite deal of wit ; a third with a talent to fing admirably ; a forth with a genious to write well in profe
and verfe. As the fifth was going to fpeak, they
heard a noife in the chimney like that of a great
ftone falling down from the top of a fteeple, and Caraboffa

bofia appeared all over in a fweat, crying out, ' And I
' alfo endow this little creature ;

> ' Mifchief fhe fhall give and take
> ' 'Till her years doth twenty make.'

The queen, who was in her bed, fell a weeping at
thefe words, and begged Carabofia to pity the poor innocent princefs. All the fairies did the fame ; faying,
' Pray, fifter, unfwarm her.' But the ugly wretch was
inexorable, and would not be perfuaded to it. So the
fifth fairy who had faid nothing, to make up the matter, endowed her with a long and happy life, after the
time of Carabofia's curfe was expired. The beldam
fairy did nothing but laugh at them, fung fome fongs
in contempt of them, and mounting her invifible car,
returned as fhe came, through the chimney. All the
fifters were in great confternation : the poor queen was
at death's door, fo clofe had Carabofia's wayward charms
ftruck her. However, fhe gave the fairies what fhe
had promifed them ; and added fome ribbons, of which
they are very fond. The courtiers made much of them ;
and the oldeft of them, when fhe went away, advifed
the queen to let the princefs be kept in fome place or
other till fhe was twenty years old, where fhe might be
feen by none, except by her woman, who fhould be commanded to keep her locked up clofely. Upon this the
king ordered a tower to be built, clofe and faft at top,
and no windows to it; with only a lamp burning within
it. The way to it was through a valley, which ran a-
long a league under ground. The nurfes and gover-
nants had every thing they wanted conveyed to them
by this dark paffage ; and every twenty paces there was
a ftrong door, and guards fet to watch. The princefs
was called Verenata, becaufe the rofe and the lily joined
in the colour of her complexion, which was as frefh and
fair as the face of the fpring. As fhe grew up fhe became
a wonder in all the perfections with which the fairies
had endowed her. The moft difficult fciences were as
foon learned by her as the moft eafy; and fhe was fo

E 6   beautiful

beautiful, and so well shaped, that the king and queen
always wept for joy when they saw her. She begged
them sometimes to stay with her, or to suffer her to go
out with them ; for she was tired, though she could not
tell why ; but they always excused themselves.

Her nurse, who had lived with her from the time of
her birth, and did not want wit, used to tell her what
the world was, and she presently comprehended it as much
as if she had seen it. The king said to the queen, ' My dear,
' Caraboffa will be deceived, and our Verenata will be happy in spite of all her predictions.' And the queen was
extremely pleased, to think how they should baulk the
mischievous fairy's malace. They had ordered Verenata's picture to be drawn, and sent several of them to
all the courts they could think of : for the time of her
releasement approached, and they resolved to marry her,
she being within four days of twenty years of age. The
court and city prepared rejoicings for the day of the princess's liberty ; and the public joy was increased by news
that king Merlin had desired her in marriage for his
son. Fanfarinet, Merlin's ambassador, arrived to demand her ; and her nurse having represented that nothing in the world was so fine as his entry would be,
the princess longed passionately to see it. ' How un-
' happy am I (said she) to be locked up in a dark tower !
' I have never seen the heavens, the sun, nor stars, of
' which I have heard such wonders : I have never seen
' a horse, an ape, or a lion, unless it be in painting.——
' The king and queen told me I should come out when
' I was twenty years old, but they only said it to amuse
' me, that I may be patient. It is plain, I am desti-
' ned to perish here, without having given offence to
' any one.' She then wept so bitterly that her eyes
swelled in her head : her nurse, her foster-sister, her
dresser and rocker, and all her women who waited upon
her, loved her entirely, and wept as much as she to see
her weep. The whole company were almost drowned
in tears, and choaked with sighs. Never was sorrow so
complete. And the princess observed that they were
all mightily concerned for her, took up a knife, threatening

threatening them, if they did not contrive some way or
other for her seeing Fanfarinet's public entry, she would
strike it to her heart. She added, neither the king or
queen should ever know it: consider with yourselves,
had you rather I should stab myself here, than give me
the satisfaction I desire of you? at these words, the nurse
and the other attendant, broke out into tears, weeping
and sighing · and they resolved they would get her an
opportunity to see Fanfarinet, or die in attempting it.——
They consulted the whole night how to bring it about,
but could not think of the means to effect it. the princess, who was eager to see the fight, animated them in
their consultations, by saying, ' Never tell me you
' love me again ; if you did, you would find out a way
' to oblige me in this one request. I have read, that
' love and friendship surmount all difficulties.' At last
they came to a resolution, to dig out a hole in the tower
on that side of the city where Fanfarinet was to make
his entry. They took down the princess's bed, and all
of them were employed night and day in the business
they had undertaken. They first scraped of the plaister,
and then took out the stones. They removed so many,
that a little hole was at last made, not so big as the eye
of a needle, through which the light appeared ; and that
was the first time she saw it ; it dazzled her, and she gazed at it continually. The women could not widen it, so
she was forced to be content with what they had done ;
and looking through it sometime, at last Fanfarinet came
by at the head of a noble train. He was mounted on a
fine horse, which danced to the sound of trumpets, and
curveted to a miracle. Before him marched six musi-
cians, playing upon flutes, and six hautboys, which answered one another by echos ; then followed trumpets and
kettle-drums. Fanfarinet had a coat on embroidred
with pearls: his plume was of carnation colour: he
could hardly be seen for ribbons and diamonds, which
were not so rare in these countries as in ours, king merlin having whole chambers full of them. In a word he
made such a shining figure, that the light did not seem
brighter in the princess's eyes. She was so struck at the

fight

fight, that fhe no longer remained miftrefs of herfelf: and having thought of it a little, fhe declared fhe would never marry any man but Fanfarinet, for it was not likely that his mafter could be fo amiable as he. She faid, her education had cured her of ambition, and it would be no hard matter for a princefs, who had been bred up in a dark tower, to retire with him to a country houfe, if they were driven to it : that fhe had rather live upon bread and water with him, than have all the rarities in the world with another. In fhort fhe fpoke fo heartily, that her women began to be more alarmed. than ever, fearing what would be the effects of her paffion. They reprefented to her the injury fhe would do her own rank, to match with one of his. But their talk was in vain : She did not harken to them, refolved to follow her own inclination when fhe had it in her power.

As foon as Fanfarinet arrived at the king's palace, the queen fent for her daughter. All the ftreets were fpread with tapeftry, and the windows crowded with ladies; fome had bafkets of flowers in their hands, others bafkets of laurels, others excellent odours, with which they fcented the air to welcome the fair princefs abroad. Her women beginning to drefs her, a dwarf knocked at the tower gate, mounted on an elephant, fent by the five good fairies who had endowed her on her birth-day. They fent her a crown and feptre, a robe of golden brocade, a petticoat of butterflies wings (a wonderful piece of work) and a cafket full of ineftimable jewels : fuch a treafure was never feen together before. The queen fwooned with aftonifhment at the fight. The princefs, on her part, took little notice of them, for all her thoughts were on Fanfarinet. The dwarf was thanked, and rewarded for his trouble with one thoufand ells of fine ribbon, of feveral colours, with which he made garters, cravat-ftrings, and hatbands.— The queen defired him to ftay till fhe had fetched fomthing for the fairies, worthy their acceptance : and the princefs, who was very generous, made them a prefent of fome german fpinning wheels, and cedar fpindles.— The rare things which the dwarf brought were made ufe of.

of to adorn her : and she appeared so surprisingly beautiful to every body who saw her, that the sun's lustre was thought to be faint to her's. She walked through the streets on rich tapestry ; and the people who flocked to behold her, cried out continually, how lovely she is, how charming !

As she marched along in this pomp and splendour, accompanied by the queen and four or five dozen of princesses of the blood, besides ten dozen more who came from the neighbouring kingdoms to assist at this feast, the sky on a sudden darkened, the thunder rumbled in the air, and rain and hail fell in torrents. The queen flung her royal robes over her head ; the ladies did the same by theirs : and Verenata was going to do it, when the sound and cry of a thousand ravens, crows, owls, and other birds of ill omen was heard, which seemed to presage that nothing good would come to this festival. At the same time a rascally owl, of a prodigious bigness, was seen flying towards the princess with a cobweb scarf in his mouth, embroidered with bats wings, which he let fall on Verenata's shoulders. He had no sooner done it, but the company heard a loud laughter, and supposed it was a scurvy trick played them by Carabossa.

Every one was grieved at this melancholy sight, and the queen more than all of them : she wept, and endeavoured to take off the black scarf from her daughter's shoulders, but it stuck as close as if it had been a part of her. 'Ah (cried she) our enemy is too hard for us 'still : nothing will appease her. I sent her fifty 'pounds of comfits, as much double refined sugar, and 'two Westphalia hams, and she is as mischievous as 'ever.'

While she was complaning thus, the princess, and all that attended her, began to be wet to their skins.— Verenata, whose head was full of the ambassador, got ground of them all in the procession, and went on without saying a word. She thought, if she had the good luck to please the man she loved, she would neither care for Carabossa nor for her scarf, though it was looked upon to be such a bid presage. She admired, within herself, why he did not come to meet her; but her admiration was at an end, when she saw him advancing by the side of the king; upon which the trumpets sounded, the drums beat, and the violins made an agreeable entertainment to the assembly, who redoubled their shouts, and their joy was as extraordinary as the occasion of it.

Fanfarinet had a great deal of wit: but when he beheld the grace, majesty, and beauty of the princess he was so transported, that instead of seriously talking when he courted her, one would have imagined he was drunk, though he drank nothing but a dish of chocolate. He become like a madman, when he perceived that with one glance he had forgot that fine harangue he had prepared for her, and which he had got so by heart, that he could before this minute repeat it in his sleep. While he was endeavouring to recollect himself, he made several low bows to the princess, who on her side also made him half a dozen courtsies, not considering what she did. At last she broke silence and to help him out of the confusion which she saw he was in, addressed herself thus to him : ‘ My lord Fanfarinet, I can easily imagine ‘ that all that you would say to me is charming; I doubt ‘ not but your wit is answerable to your character: Let ‘ us however make haste to the palace ; it rains like ‘ a deluge: and Carabossa, who owes us this ill turn, ‘ will not spare us till we get thither.’ Fanfarinet replied very gallantly, ‘ The fairy had very wisely provided ‘ rain, to quench the fires which those bright eyes would. ‘ light.’ He then took her by the hand, and led her forward As they were walking, she said to him softly, ‘ You will ‘ not guess at the opinion I have of you, unless I explain ‘ myself further, ; it is true, I cannot do it without ‘ pain ; but, *Honi soit qui mal y pense*, Evil be to them ‘ that evil think. Know then, my lord Ambassador, ‘ that I have beheld you with wonder, and was surprised at the charming figure you made on horseback at ‘ your public entry, when the horse danced and curveted ; I am sorry you came hither on any other man’s account. If you have as much courage as I to find out

an

' an expedient for it, instead of marrying you in your
' master's name, I will marry you in your own.   I
' know you are not a prince; what then ? I like you as
' well as if you were : we'll fly together to some corner
' of the world ; we shall be blamed at first ; no matter,
' others may do worse ; and when people are weary of
' blaming us, they will leave us in quiet to enjoy our
' retirement, where I shall be glad to be with you.'

Fanfarinet thought he dreamt, for Verenata was a
princess of admirable qualities and perfections, that he
could never have hoped for that honour, unless some
strange whimsy had seized her.   He had not presence of
mind enough to answer her; had they been alone, he
would have thrown himself at her feet; he now could
only clasp her hand, which he did so closely, that he hurt
her little finger, yet she did not cry out : so much her
passion ran in her head, that she was insensible of any
thing else.   When she entered the palace, a thousand
of several sorts of musical instruments were tuned for
her welcome, to which were added a concert of such
heavenly voices, that the audience were afraid of brea-
thing, lest they should make too much noise, and so
interrupt the harmony.   The king having kissed his
daughter's forehead and cheeks, spoke to her as follows :
' my pretty lambkin (for he was used to give her such
little tender names) are not you glad you are going to
' marry the great king Merlin's son ? the Lord Fanfari-
' net, whom you see here, is come to perform the cere-
' mony, and will carry you into the finest kingdom in
' the world ?   The princess courtesied down to the
ground, and answered, ' I shall obey you, father, in all
' things with pleasure, if my dear mamma will consent
' to it.'   The princess was bred up in so much tenderness to her parents, that she had not forgot the pretty
terms she used in her leading strings ; ' I consent (says her
mother) with all my heart,   (and embraced her as a
token of her joy.)   ' Let dinner be got ready immedi-
' ately,' (quoth the queen.)   It was no sooner said, but
an hundred tables were spread in an instant, and all the
company fell too hartily, except Verenata and Fanfarinet, who looked at one another so much, that they had
no time for eating, nor thinking upon any thing else.—

After the feaſt there was a ball and a play : but it was
ſo late before they had done ſupper, and they had eat ſo
plentifully, that moſt of the people of quality, and others
who were there, ſlept as they ſat.   Their majeſties themſelves fell into a ſound nap on a couch ; the lords and
ladies ſnored again, and the fidlers nodded over their
inſtruments, and knew not what they did.   Our lovers
were the only perſons that were well awake : and ſeeing
they were not obſerved, toyed as lovers are uſed to do
when they have an opportunity to ſhew their paſſions.
Verenata perceiving the guards, as well as the reſt, were
aſleep, ſaid to Fanfarinet, ‘ this minute is ours ; let us
‘ improve it and be gone ; if we ſtay till the marriage
‘ ceremony is over, the king will place ſome ladies of
‘ the court about me, and order a prince to accompany
‘ me to your maſter’s court ; it is better for us to take
‘ hold of the preſent opportunity than to wait for ano-
‘ ther.’   She then roſe up, and took the king’s dagger
from his ſide, which was all over ſet in diamonds.   She
alſo carried away with her the queen’s mantle, which
ſhe had laid by, to ſleep the more at her eaſe, in which
was a carbuncle of ineſtimable value, and a diamond
that rendered the perſon who wore it inviſible.   Fanfarinet took her by her lily white hand, and bending one
knee to the ground, replied, ‘ I ſwear by all that is held
‘ ſacred in heaven or earth, that I will eternally be
‘ faithful and obedient to your highneſs : you do
‘ every thing for me madam, and can there be any thing
‘ that I will not do for you ?’ They then went both of
them out of the palace, the ambaſſador taking a dark
lanthorn in his hand.   They paſſed through ſeveral
bye-ſtreets and lanes, till they came to the ſea-ſide,
where they took a boat.   Their mariner was a poor old
fellow who lay aſleep in his bark.   They wak d
him ; and when he ſaw Verenata ſo beautiful and glitter-
ing with jewels, with the black batt-feather ſcarf on her
ſhoulders, he took her for the goddeſs of night, and fell
down to worſhip her.   The lovers had no time for cere-
monies ; they commanded him to put to ſea, which he
was not over willing to do, for there was neither moon

nor.

nor ftars to be feen, the weather being ftill cloudy, occafioned by the tempeft Caraboffa had raifed. It is true, there was a carbuncle on the queen's mantle, which fhone more than fifty lighted torches, and Fanfarinet might, as we are told, have faved himfelf the trouble of carrying a dark lanthorn with him. The ambaffador afked the princefs whither fhe would go? 'Alas (faid fhe) ' I will go along with you ; wherever you will go, I will ' go ; I think of nothing elfe.' 'But, madam,, (quoth Fanfarinet) I dare not conduct you to the court of king ' Merlin ; it is as much as my neck is worth to be ' caught within his dominions. Well then (replied Verenata) let us go to the defert ifle of Squirrels; it is ' far enough off, and we need not fear being followed ' thither,' She ordered the mariner to fet fail ; and though his bark was of a very fmall fize, he obeyed her.

As day began to break, the king, queen, and court, having fhook their ears and rubbed their eyes a little, got up, intending to finifh the folemnity of the princefs's marriage. The queen haftily called for her mantle, and fearch was directly made after it, from the clofet to the kitchen, but no mantle was to be found. Then her majefty went herfelf to feek it, ran up ftairs and down ftairs into the cellar and garret, but no tidings could be heard of it.

The king alfo in his turn was willing to adjuft him-felf, and in order to it to put his bright dagger by his fide, which being miffing, as well as the mantle royal, half the court were employed to fearch for it ; boxes and coffers were opened, whofe infide had not feen the fun in an hundred years. A thoufand rarities were found, puppets that could turn about their heads and eyes, gol-den fheep with their little lambs, fweet-meats and com-fits: but no dagger ; fo the king was inconfolable ; he tore his reverend beard, and the queen her hair to keep him company. Indeed the lofs was great, for the mantle and dagger were worth more than ten cities as big as London.

When the king defpared of finding what they had loft, he took heart, and faid to the queen, ' courage my
dear

'dear, let us finish the solemnity of our daughter's nup-
'tials, which has already cost us so dear.' He asked
where the princess was? her nurse came up and told
him, that she had been seeking her above two hours,
and could not find her. This bad news so increased
the king and his consort's trouble, that they could not
support themselves under it. The queen cried out like
an eagle that had lost her young, and fell into a swoon.
And never was a more melancholy sight; above two
pails of hungary water were thrown upon her majesty's
face before they could fetch her to life again. The ladies and maids of honour wept as if they had been at a
funeral, and not at a wedding. The servants came one
and all, in a doleful tone, saying, 'What, is the king's
'daughter lost?' And the king seeing she was not to be
found, bade his page look out Fanfarinet, who doubtless,
says he is sleeping in one corner of the room or other,
and let him come and grive with us. The page sought
after him every where, and could hear no more tidings
of him than of the mantle and dagger. This misfortune was another affliction to their majesties, who
in truth had enough before to render them the most dis-
consolate couple on earth.

The king summoned all the councellors and officers,
civil and military, to attend him in the great hall of
the palace, where he and his queen, who we may perceive was a considerable person in the government,
went to them clad in deep mourning. Their rich robes
being thrown off, each of them had a black gown on,
tied round with a rope, to express the greatness of their
sorrows. When the assembly saw them in this lamen-
table condition, the hall resounded with sighs and groans,
and the floor was overwhelmed with floods of tears.—
The king, who had not time enough to prepare a speech,
suitable to the occasion, was silent three hours. At
length he opened his majestic mouth and spoke as follows.

Hear, little and great; hear your king, and help him with
your advice. I have lost my dear daughter Verenata, and
know not whether she is destroyed or stolen from me; the queen's
mantle

*mantle and my dagger, which are worth more than their
weight in gold, are also gone; and what is worst of all, the
ambassador Fanfarinet is not to be found. It is to be feared,
when the king his master is informed of this accident, he will
come and seek after him, and charge us with cutting him as
small as minced meat, for a christmas pye. I should not take
it so much to heart, if I had money to spare; but I must confess
to you plainly, the charges of the wedding have undone me.—
Tell me, my dear subjects, what shall I do, and what means you
would have me make use of to retrieve my daughter, Fanfarinet,
the mantle, and the dagger.*

Every body admired the king's eloquent speech, he
never made so florid a one in his life; and my lord
Gambello, chancellor of the kingdom, in the name of
the assembly, replied thus, not bating him an ace in eloquence:

SIR,
*We are all sorry for your sorrow, and would rather have
parted with our wives and children, than you should have had so
much cause to grieve; but it is plain, this is a trick of Carabossa
the fairy: the princess's twentieth year is not yet expired;
and since I must speak my sentiments, or your majesty suffer by
my double-dealings with you, I freely declare, that I observed
she was always ogling Fanfarinet, and he her. Perhaps love
has been playing one of his pranks, as often happens with persons of their ages.*

The queen, who was naturally hasty, interrupted the
chancellor, saying, ' Have a care what you say, my
' lord chancellor; the princess, I would have you to
' know, is no such sort of person as to fall in love
' with Fanfarinet; I have bred her up too well for that.'
Then the nurse, who was one of the company, fell at
the king's feet, and said; ' I am come to tell your ma-
' jesties the whole truth of the matter. The princess
' swore she would see Fanfarinet make his public entry,
' or stab herself on the spot: we made a little hole in
' the tower through which she saw him, and immediately

' ately protested she would never marry any man but
' him.' The assembly hearing this, were extremely
troubled at Verenata's folly and fortune: they saw that
Gambello's penetration was greater than her majesty's;
who all in a rage, scolded at Verenata's nurse, and dresser, rocker, foster-sister and companion, so terribly,
that hanging would hardly have been a worse punishment. Admiral Sharp-Cap interrupting the queen,
cried out, ' My lords, let's after Fanfarinet, for without
' doubt this jackanapes has carried off our princess.'—
Every body clapped their hands in applause of their admiral, and there was not a man but said he would follow him. Some of them went by sea, and others by
land, who traveling from kingdom to kingdom, with
drums beating and trumpets sounding, made proclamation, 'That whoever could tell tale or tidings of the
' princess Verenata, whom Fanfarinet had stolen
' out of her father's palace, should have for their reward
' a fine baby, some sweet-meats wet and dry, some
' little scissars, a gown made of cloth of gold, and a sa-
' tin bonnet.' The answer every where was, ' You must
' go somewhere else, we know nothing of them.'

Those who went by sea were more fortunate; for,
after a pretty long voyage, they one night perceived
something before them which shone like a great fire,
but were afraid of coming up near to it, not knowing
what it was; when all on a sudden the light stopped at
the desert isle of Squirrels, for it was indeed the princess's
carbuncle that was so luminous: and she and her lover
landing there gave the mariner one hundred crowns of
gold, bid him farewell, and charged him for his life not
to speak a word to any one what ever of his adventure.

The good man in his way back, met the king's ships,
which he no sooner saw but he endeavoured to avoid
them. The admiral perceived it, ordered a galley to
give him chace, and the old man was too weak to row
from her. So the admiral's men came up with him,
took him, and carried him before their commander, who
caused him to be secured, and the hundred pieces of
gold being found in his pocket, the very same pieces that
had

had been coined in honour of the princefs's nuptials,.
Sharp-cap examined him : and the mariner, that he
might not be obliged to fpeak the truth, affected to appear deaf and dumb. ‘ So, fo (fays the admiral) we;
‘ fhall foon bring him to his tongue, I will warrant ye.'
So he commanded him to be tied to the main maft :
and exercifed with a cat o'nine-tails ; one of the beft re-
medies in the world for mutes. When the old man
faw they were in earneft, he confeffed that a heavenly
creature, in the fhape of a young lady, and a gallant
gentleman, had hired his boat to convey them to the
defert ifle of Squirrels. The admiral imagined prefently it was the princefs and Fanfarinet, and failed to that
ifland in purfuit of them.

In the mean time Verenata, tired with the fatigue of.
the fea, and finding a green bank under a covert of trees,
laid down and fell afleep. Fanfarinet whofe ftomach was
fharper than his love, did not let her fleep long. ‘ Do
‘ you think, madam, (fays he waking her) that I can
‘ ftay here for ever ? I do not fee any thing that
‘ is eatable upon the place: though you were fairer
‘ than Aurora, that would not fatisfy my hunger ; one
‘ muft have fome nourifhment, or there is no living ;
‘ my ftomach's fharp, and my belly empty.' ‘How !
(replied Verenata ;) do the marks that I have given you
‘ of my friendfhip go for nothing with you ; is it poffi-
‘ ble your mind can be biaffed about any thing but the
‘ contemplation of your good fortune ?' ‘ It is rather ta-
‘ ken up (faid Fanfarinet) about my bad ; would to
‘ heaven you were in your black tower again.' ‘Do
‘ not be fo out of humour, my good cavelier (quoth the
princefs, fmiling) ‘ I will go fearch the woods, and per-
‘ haps I may light upon fome fruit to fatisfy you.' —
‘ I had rather you might find a wolf to eat you (replied
Fanfarinet, churlifhly.') Verenata, as fhe afterwards faid,
went up and down the woods, tearing her robes among
the briars, and her white fkin with the thorns, fhe was
fcratched as if fhe had been playing with cats. And thus it
is, if young women will fall in love with young fellows,
there is nothing but trouble comes of it. When fhe had
                                          fearched

searched every where in vain, she returned very sorrowful to Fanfarinet and told him the uncomfortable news. He turned his back upon her, and left her, muttering between his teeth.

The next day they looked about for some eatables as unsuccessfully as the first; so that they were forced for three days together to live upon leaves and locusts——Though the princess had been, without comparison, much more delicately bred than the ambassador, yet she did not complain. ' I should be content, (said she to her lover) if I suffered alone, and would be willing to ' die of hunger if I could procure some good cheer for ' you.' ' It is all one to me (quoth Fanfarinet) whe- ' ther you live or die, provided I have what I want.'— ' Is it possible (cried Verenata) that you should be so ' little concerned at my death ? are these the oaths which ' you swore when you left my father's court ?' ' There ' is a great deal of difference (says the ambassador) be- ' tween a man at his ease, who has neither hunger nor ' thirst, and a wretch ready to be starved.' She ans- ' wered, I am in as much danger as you, and I do not ' complain.' ' You may well bear it with a good grace, (says Fanfarinet) who was so mad as to leave father ' and mother, to run up and down here like a vagabond; ' we are in a very pretty condition truly :' ' It is for ' love of you (replied Verenata) and at the same time gave him her hand. ' I would have excused you, (said Fan- farinet) had I known what you would have brought me ' to ;' and then turned aside from her. The fair prin- cess, overwhelmed with grief, wept incessantly, enough to have softened a heart of flint with her tears, She sat under a bush loaded with roses, white and red, to which she thus addressed herself, after she had for some time gazed upon them : ' How blessed are you, ye ' young flowers; the zephyrs caress, the dew waters, the ' sun beautifies, the bees love you, your prickles defend ' you, and all the world admire you ; must you alas be ' more happy than I !' She then fell a weeping so ex- cessively, that the root of the rose tree was moistened with her tears ; and she had scarce done speaking, before, to

5   her

her great furprife, the bufh ftirred, the flowers blew,
and the faireft of them anfwered her thus ; ' If thou
' hadft never loved, thy deftiny would have been to be
' envied as much as mine; love expofes people to the
' worft misfortunes. Poor princefs, look in the hollow
' of this tree, and you'll find a honeycomb, but do not
' be fo filly as to give it to Fanfarinet.' Verenata rofe
immediately, not knowing whether fhe was afleep or
awake ; fearched the tree, found the hole, and honey in
it, which fhe prefently carried to her ungrateful lover.
' Here, fays fhe, is a honeycomb, for you : I might have
' eat it all myfelf, but I had rather fhare it with you.'
The ambaffador fnatched it out of her hand, without fo
much as thanking her, or looking upon her, eat it all
up, and refufed to give her the leaft bit. He was fuch a
brute as to infult her, by faying it was too fweet for her,
and would fpoil her teeth ; with feveral other imperti-
nent jefts. Verenata, more forrowful than ever, fat
down under an oak, and made much the fame fort of
complaint as fhe had made to the rofe tree. The oak,
touched with compaffion, bowed down fome of its branches, and fpoke to this purpofe, (for it was all enchanted-
ground that fhe trod upon:) ' It is a pity, fair Verenata,
' you fhould die fo young : take this pitcher of milk and
' drink it, without giving a drop to your ungrateful lover.'
The princefs, more aftonifhed than before, looked behind
her, and fpied a great pitcher of milk. She forgot her
own thirft prefently, and remembered Fanfarinet, whom
fhe believed might well be thirfty after eating about
fifteen pounds of honey ; fo fhe ran to him with the
milk, bidding him quench his thirft, and remember to
fave her fome, for fhe was almoft dead for want of it.—
He took the pitcher rudely from her, drank it off every
drop, flung the pitcher to the ground, and broke it to
pieces, faying, with a malicious fmile. ' Thofe that
' have had no meat need no drink.'

The princefs lifted up her hands and bright eyes to
heaven, cried out, 'It is juft ye powers ! I have deferved
' this punifhment for leaving my father and mother
' to love, and follow a man whom I never knew, with-

F

out

' out considering my duty to my parents, and my rank,
' or thinking on the miseries which Caraboffa threatened
' me with.' After she had done speaking she wept
more bitterly than she had done all her life time, and
retired into the thickest of the wood, where out of mere
faintness she fell down at the foot of an elm, on which a
nightingale perched, and sung so wonderfully sweet,
that her notes had almost charmed the wretched Verenata with pleasure. The bird, like the tree, had the gift
of speech, and fluttering its wings, repeated these verses,
which it had learnt on purpose out of Ovid, as if it had
understood the princess's distemper, and had brought her
a cure:

Cupid's *a knave, the traitor never smiles,*
But when he would enslave us by his wiles:
And ever, with his favours he imparts
A deadly poison, that torments our hearts.

' Who knows him better than I ? (answered Verenata,
interrupting the bird :) I am too well acquainted with
' his cruelty and my evil destiny.' Take heart (says
the amorous nightingale ;) under yonder plant you will
' find some sugar-plumbs and almonds, but do not be
' so foolish as to give any of them to Fanfarinet.'—
The princess did not want that precaution now ; she
had not forgot the two last tricks he played her ; besides
she was so very hungry that she needed not many arguments to persuade her to eat when she had got food. So
she cracked the almonds, eat the plumbs, and feasted
on them by herself. Fanfarinet seeing her eat alone,
fell in a furious passion : his eyes flashed fire, and he
ran with his sword drawn to kill her : she, to defend herself, exposed the miraculous diamond, and so became
invisible to him ; she got out of his way, and reproached
him with his ingratitude, in terms that shewed suffici-
ently that she could not yet hate him.
In the mean time admiral Sharp-Cap dispatched a-
way John Prattlebox, courier in ordinary of the closet,
to inform the king, that the princess and Fanfarinet,
were

were landed on the ifle of Squirrels, but that being a ftranger in the country, he was cautious of making a decent for fear of ambufcades. Upon this news, which was joyful tidings to their majefties and their court, the king fent for a huge book, every leaf of which was eight ells long; It was the mafter-piece of a learned fairy, and contained a defcription of the whole world. The king found out in an inftant that the ifle of Squirrels was not inhabited. 'Go, (fays he to John Prattlebox) ' and command the admiral in my name to land imme- ' diately; it may be of ill confequence to leave Fanfa- ' rinet and my daughter fo long together.

As foon as the Courier arrived at the fleet, the admi- ral ordered the trumpets to found, the drums to beat; cymbals, hautboys, flutes, violins, viols, organs, guitars, and a confufed variety of inftruments were played upon; which alarmed the princefs and her lover, who was not very brave. Fanfarinet fceing the danger that approached, made his peace, in hopes of affiftance from his miftrefs; who was too readily reconciled to him. ' Stand behind me (quoth Verenata) I will go before, ' hide you with my invifible diamond, and kill our ' enemies with my father's dagger, while you flay them ' with your fword.'

The invifible princefs advanced againft the foldiers, and fhe and Fanfarinet flew them all without being feen by them. Nothing was heard but cries; the poor foldiers drew their fwords in vain, they fought with the air, while every blow the ambaffador and Verenata ftruck gave certain death; and every where fuch lamen- table groans as thefe were heard, ' Oh! I am killed: Oh! I die!' The two invifible lovers fought as fafe as if they had to do with a flock of geefe; they dropt down like ducks, avoided their enemies blows, and eafily de- ftroyed them. The admiral, obferving how his men fell by unfeen hands, founded a retreat and returned very melancholy to hold a council of war.

Night drawing on apace, the princefs and Fanfarinet retired into the thickeft of the wood; She was fo weary, that fhe lay down on the grafs, and had almoft

F 2

dropt

dropt asleep, when she heard a voice whispering to her, ' Save yourself, Verenata, for Fanfarinet will kill and ' eat you.' She opened her eyes, and by the light of the carbuncle she spied the wretch Fanfarinet with his arm lifted up ready to run his sword to her heart: for perceiving her skin was so white, and her flesh so plump, his hunger inspired him with other thoughts than love, and the opportunity might have put it into his head ; he had a mind to make a meal of her, and intended to murder her for that purpose. Verenata did not stand long deliberating what she should do ; she drew out her dagger gently, having kept it for her own use ever since the battle, and stabbed him so very fiercely in the eye that he fell down dead. ' Go, ingrate, she cried, take ' the last favour, which thou hast best deserved from me ; ' be an example for the future, to all faithless lovers, ' and may thy disloyal heart never find rest in the world ' to which I have sent thee.

When the first transport of her passion was over, and she reflected on the condition she was in, she had almost as little life in her, as the man whom she had just slain. ' What will become of me, (said she weeping) I am left ' alone in this desolate island ; the wild beasts will either ' devour me, or I shall die with hunger.' She was even sorry that she had not suffered Fanfarinet to eat her, rather than expose herself to be eaten by the monsters of the desert ; she sat down trembling, and wishing for morning.

As she rested herself against a tree, she espied on one side of her a golden chariot, drawn by six great hens with cropped crowns. A cock was the coachman, and a fat hen the postillion. In the chariot there rode a lady, so fair, that the sun lost all his lustre, wherever she shone, and night illuminated by her eyes, was brighter than meridian day. Her robe was all over set with spangles of silver and gold. On the other side of her Verenata saw another chariot drawn by six bats ; a crow was the coachman, and a beetle the postillion. Within the chariot sat a little frightful hag, cloathed with snakes-skin garment, and on her head she wore a great toad, which served her instead of a top-knot.

Never

Never was a woman more furprifed than the young
princefs was at this fight : while fhe ftood gazing upon
it, fhe faw the two chariots advance againft each other,
The beautiful lady held a golden lance in her hand, and
the ugly one an old rufty fpear. They came up fiercely
to the combat, which lafted a quarter of an hour. At
laft the fair heroine got the victory, and the deformed
hag fled with her bats. The battle being over, the
handfome lady defcended to the earth, and thus addreffed herfelf to Verenata :

Fear nothing lovely princefs ; I come hither only to
oblige you ; I fought with Caraboffa out of love to you ;
fhe pretended to an authority to whip you, becaufe you
came out of the tower four days before your twentieth
year expired. You fee I took your part, and have driven her away ; rejoice at the happinefs I bring you.——
The grateful princefs fell proftrate at her feet, and
made this anfwer: ‘ Great queen of the fairies, I am
‘ tranfported at your generofity, and cannot find words
‘ to exprefs my gratitude: but this I know, that there
‘ is not a drop of that blood which you have faved, which
‘ I am not ready to facrifice for your fervice.’ The
fairy embraced her twice, and by her fpells rendered
her, if it was poffible, more beautiful than fhe was before. She commanded the cock, her coachman, to go
to the king's fhip, and bid the admiral come to the
princefs, for there was nothing now that he need be a-
fraid of; and her poftillion the hen, to her own palace,
to fetch fome new robes for Verenata, which were the
richeft that ever eyes were fet upon.

The admiral was fo ravifhed with the news which the
cock brought him, that it was like to have thrown him
into a fit of ficknefs : he landed immediately in the
ifland, taking all his men with him ; and among the
reft Jack Prattlebox, the exprefs that arrived lately from
court, who feeing every one run afhore did the fame,
and carried along with him a fpit with wild fowl upon
it half roafted.

Admiral Sharp-Cap had fcarce gone a league before
he faw the chariot drawn by hens in a great road in the

wood

wood, and the two ladies walking together. He knew
the princefs, and bowed to the ground, was going to
begin a notable fpeech. Verenata, interrupting him,
faid, ' All thofe honours were due to the generous fairy,
' who defended her from Caraboffa's clutches.' Upon
this the admiral kiffed the hem of her fairy majefty's
garment, and made her one of the fineft compliments
that ever came out of the mouth of a tar on fuch an occafion. While he was talking to her, the princefs cried
out, ' Certainly I fmell roaft meat. Yes, madam, (replied Prattlebox, and produced his fpit with the birds
on it,) your ladyfhip never eat better in your life.' ' I
' am very glad ot it (quoth the fairy) though not fo
' much on my own account as on the princefs's, who
' wants fome refrefhment.' The admiral fent away to
his fhips for other neceffaries : and the joy of his whole
crew for his finding the princefs, joined with their good
cheer, made them all wonderful merry.

The feaft being over, and the fat hen returned, the
fairy dreffed the princefs in a robe of green filk, brocaded
with gold, fet with rubies and pearls ; fhe bound up her
hair locks with ftrings of jewels and emeralds ; fhe crowned
her with garlands of flowers, and placed her in the chariot ; where, as fhe rode, all the ftars that faw her, took
her for the morning, and faluted her as fhe paffed by,
crying, ' Good morrow, Aurora.

The fairy carried her to the fea-fide ; when they arrived there, they bid one another many a hearty adieu,
' Ah, madam (faid the princefs) will you not let me tell
' my mother to whom I owe this mighty obligation ?'
' The fairy anfwered, Embrace her on my behalf, and
' tell her I am the fifth fairy that endowed you at your
birth.'

The princefs going aboard, the admiral commanded
all the cannon to be fired ; and welcomed her with a
volley of fmall arms. The fleet returned fafely to the
port of her father's capital city ; and when fhe landed, the
king and queen, who waited on the fhore for her coming,
received her with fuch tranfport of joy, that they did not
give her time to beg pardon for her paft extravagancies,
                                                    though

though she had thrown herself at their feet as soon as she saw them. Their parental tenderness laid all the fault on Caraboffa ; and the princess was excused, as acting by an irresistible impulse of fate.

At the same time the great king Merlin's son arrived, very much troubled that he heard no news of his ambassador. He had a train of one thousand horse, and thirty pages richly dressed in scarlet liveries, embroidered and laced with gold : he was an hundred times handsomer than the ungrateful wretch Fanfarinet. Care was taken not to let him know any thing of his flight, and the princess's, because that might have created suspicions which would have shocked a lover. He was told very gravely, that the ambassador being dry, went to draw water out of a well, fell into it, and was drowned.—His highness believed every word of it ; was married to the princess ; and the joy of the whole court was so great, that they quite forgot their late sorrow.

Ye lovers, be your objects what they will,
Keep ye within the rules of duty still :
And never be by passion led away,
So much, but reason still shall have the sway :
Let her restrain the rage of your desires,
And make her mistress of your vows and fires.

THE.

THE

STORY

OF

FLORIO and FLORELLA.

THERE was a country-woman, who, upon her intimacy with a fairy, defired her to come and affift at her labour. The good woman was delivered of a daughter: when, the fairy taking the infant in her arms, faid to the mother, ' Make your choice: the child (if you have a mind) fhall be exquifitely handfome ; ' excell in wit, even more than in beauty ; and be the ' queen of a mighty empire; but withal unhappy ; or (if you had rather) fhe fhall be an ordinary, ugly, country ' creature, like yourfelf ; but contented with her condi- ' tion.' The mother immediately chofe wit and beauty for her daughter ; at the hazard of any misfortune.

As the child grew, new beauties opened daily in her face : till in a few years, fhe furpaffed all the rural laffes that the oldeft people had ever feen. Her turn of wit was gentle, polite, and infinuating : fhe was of a ready apprehenfion ; and foon learned every thing, fo as to excel her teachers. Every holiday fhe danced upon the green, with a fuperior grace to any of her companions. Her voice was fweeter than any fhepherd's pipe ; and fhe made the fongs fhe ufed to fing.

For

For some time, she was not apprifed of her own charms ; when, diverting herfelf with her playfellows, on the green flowery border of a fountain ; she was furprifed with the reflection of her face : she obferved, how different her features and her complexion feemed from the reft of her company ; and admired herfelf. The country, flocked from day to day to obtain a fight of her; made her yet more fenfible of her beauty. Her mother, who relied on the predictions of the fairy, began already to treat her as a queen, and fpoiled her with flatteries. The young damfel would neither few nor fpin, nor look after the fheep : her whole amufement was, to gather flowers, to drefs her hair with them, to fing, and to dance in the fhade.

The king of the country was a very powerful king : and he had but one fon; whofe name was Florio : for which reafon, his father was impatient to have him married. The young prince could never bear the mentioning any of the princeffes of the neighbouring nations ; becaufe a fairy had told him, that he fhould find a fhepherdefs more beautiful, and more accomplished than all the princeffes in the world. Therefore the king gave orders to affemble all the village nymphs of his realm, who where under the age of eighteen, to make a choice of her, who fhould appear worthy of fo great an honour. In purfuance of the order, when they came to be forted; a vaft number of virgins, whofe beauty was not very extraordinary, were refufed admittance ; and only thirty picked out, who infinitely furpaffed all others. Thefe thirty virgins, were ranged in a great hall, in the figure of a half moon : that the king and his fon might have a diftinct view of them together. Florello (our young damfel) appeared in the midft of her competitors, like a lily amidft marygolds ; or, as an orange-tree in bloffom, fhews amongft the mountain fhrubs. The king immediately declared aloud, that fhe deferved his crown : and Florio thought himfelf happy in the poffeffion of Florella.

Our fhepherdefs was inftantly defired to caft off her country weeds and to accept a habit richly embroidered
with

with gold. In a few minutes, fhe faw herfelf covered
with pearls and diamonds ; and a troop of ladies were
appointed to ferve her. Every one was attentive to prevent her defires, before fhe fpoke; and fhe was lodged
within the palace, in a magnificent apartment: where
inftead of tapeftry, there were large pannels of looking-
glafs, from the floor to the ceiling ; that fhe might have
the pleafure of feeing her beauty multiplied on all fides ;
and that the prince might admire her, wherever he
caft his eyes. Florio, in a few days, quitted the chace,
and all the manly ex rcifes in which before he delighted ;
that he might be perpetually with his miftrefs. The
nuptials were concluded : and foon after, the old king
died. Thereupon, Florella becoming queen, all the
councils and affairs of ftate were directed by her wifdom.
: The queen-mother (whofe name was Invideffa) grew
jealous of her daughter in-law. She was on artful, per-
verfe, cruel woman ; and age had fo much aggravated
her natural deformity, that fhe feemed a fury. The
youth and beauty of Florella, made her appear yet more
frightful ; fhe could not bear the fight of fo fine a creature : fhe likewife dreaded her wit and underftanding ;
and gave herfelf up to all the rage of envy. 'You
' want the foul of a prince (would fhe often fay to her
fon) or you would not have married this mean cottager.
' How can you be fo abject as to make an idol of her ?
' Then, fhe is as haughty as if fhe had been born in the
' palace where fhe lives. You fhould have followed the
' example of the king your father; when he thought of
' taking a wife, he prefered me, becaufe I was the daugh-
' ter of a monarch, equal to himfelf. Send away this
' infignificant fhepherdefs to her hamlet, and take to
' your bed and throne, fome young princefs, whofe birth
' is anfwerable to your own.'
Florio continued deaf to the inftances of his mother :
but one morning, Invideffa got a billet into her hands,
which Florella had writ to the king; this fhe gave to a
young courtier, who by her inftructions, fhewed t to
the king ; pretending to have received a letter from his
queen, with fuch marks of affection, as were due only
to his majefty. Florio blinded by his jealoufy, and the

malignant

malignant insinuations of his mother, immediately ordered Florella to be imprisoned for life, in a high tower,
built on the point of a rock, that stood in the sea.—
There she wept night and day; not knowing for what
supposed crime she was so severely treated by the king,
who had so passionately loved her. She was permitted
to see no person but an old woman, to whom Invidessa
had intrusted her; and whose business it was to insult
her upon all occasions.

Now Florella called to mind the village, the cottage,
the sweet privacy, and the rural pleasures she had quitted. One day as she sat in a pensive posture, overwhelmed with grief, and to herself accused the folly of
her mother, who chose rather to have her a beautiful
unfortunate queen, than an ugly contented shepherdess;
the old woman, who was her tormentor, came to acquaint her that the king had sent an executioner to
take off her head; and that she must prepare to die. —
Florella replied, that she was ready to receive the stroke.
Accordingly, the executioner sent by the king's order,
at the persuasions of Invidessa, appeared with a drawn
sabre in his hand, ready to perform his commission;
when a woman stepped in, who said, she came from the
queen-mother, to speak a word or two in p ivate to Florella,
before she was put to death. The old woman imagining
her to be one of the ladies of the court, suffered her to
deliver her message; but it was the fairy, who had foretold the misfortunes of Florella at her birth; and had
now assumed the likeness of one of Invidessa's attendants.

She desired the company to retire a while; and then
spoke thus to Florella in secret; 'Are you willing to
' renounce that beauty, which has proved so fatal to you?
' are you willing to quit the title of queen; to put on
' your former habit, and to return to your village?'—
Florella was transported at the offer. Thereupon the
fairy applied an enchanted vizard to her face · her features instantly became deformed; all the symmetry
vanished, and she was now as disagreeable as she had
been handsome. Under this change, it was not possible
to know her; and she passed without difficulty, through

the

the company who came to fee her execution. In vain did they fearch the tower ; Florella was not to be found. the news of this efcape was foon brought to the king, and to Invideſſa, who commanded diligent fearch to be made after her throughout the kingdom ; but to no pur-pofe.

The fairy by this time, had reſtored Florella to her mother ; who would never have been able to recollect her altered looks, had ſhe not been let into the circum-ſtances of her ſtory. Our ſhepherdefs was now conten-ted to live an ugly, poor unknown creature, in the village where ſhe tended ſheep. She frequently heard people relate, and lament over her adventures; fongs were made upon them, which drew tears from all eyes: ſhe often took a pleafure in finging thofe fongs, with her companions, and would often weep with the reſt: but ſtill, ſhe thought herfelf happy, with her little flock ; and was never once tempted to difcover herfelf to any of her acquaintance.

After all the care and attendance of the fairy upon the unfortunate Florella, ſhe did not forget amply to reward the queen-mother, who was the principal inſtru-ment of her darling's unhapinefs. And therefore to compenfate, in fome meafure, for her misfortunes, ſhe infpired the king's chief miniſter with notions that his artful and cruel mother had formed a defign to take the government into her own hands, and wed with a pow-erful monarch, whofe difpofition perfectly correfponded with her own. Enraged at the information, he called together fome of his nobles, to confult thereon, who gave it as their opinion, that ſhe deferved death ; but as the ties of nature prevented it, her fon commanded her to be placed in that tower from whence his once loved Florella had efcaped, where ſhe fpent the remainder of her life.

The M O R A L.

This tale ſhews the folly of wiſhing to be in any ſtate of life for which we were not defigned, and that true happinefs confiſts in being eafy and content.